All-American

Also by John R. Tunis

IRON DUKE

THE DUKE DECIDES

CHAMPION'S CHOICE

THE KID FROM TOMKINSVILLE

WORLD SERIES

KEYSTONE KIDS

ROOKIE OF THE YEAR

YEA! WILDCATS!

A CITY FOR LINCOLN

All-American

JOHN R. TUNIS

An Odyssey Classic
Harcourt Brace Jovanovich, Publishers
San Diego   New York   London

Library of Congress Cataloging-in-Publication Data

Tunis, John Roberts, 1889–1975
All-American/John R. Tunis.
p.   cm.
"An Odyssey classic."
Summary: After he and a fellow player on the football field gang up on a Jewish
member of the opposing team and cause him a serious neck injury, seventeen-year-
old Ronny leaves his elite all-white private school for the integrated public high
school, where he discovers that the practice of democracy takes courage and loyalty
to one's principles.
ISBN 0-15-202292-9 (pbk.)
[1. Football—Fiction.   2. Schools—Fiction.   3. Prejudices— Fiction.]   I. Title.
PZ7.T8236A1   1989
[Fic]—dc19   89-2075

Printed in the United States of America

A B C D E

Introduction

If *A City for Lincoln* is an enigmatic title, *All-American* seems clear enough. It is a familiar label for any athlete who has been selected as one of the nation's best. At the beginning and end of every major sports season in high school and college, dozens of All-American rosters are assembled from teams all over the country, like menus of nothing but desserts: the greatest quarterback in a backfield with the greatest fullback, behind the greatest linemen, and so on. A kid who makes All-American will carry that confection of a designation with him or her forever, as a promise that has been either kept or unfulfilled.

This book is the story of an athlete, a football player named Ronny who stars for a prep school, quits the institution when his teammates strike an arrogant note of elitism over public school kids, and goes on to star in sports and what we used to call "citizenship" at the public school. It is a terrific sports story, and Ronny is indeed a great player. But nowhere is there any reference to the honorific menu-making the title implies. Ronny makes no All-American teams; in fact, there is no reference whatever to this particular honor.

Did Tunis forget something? Shouldn't the novel end with Ronny winning a big game and receiving the nod from *Sports Illustrated* or Kodak or the National Association of High School Coaches? Instead, it ends with Ronny's team receiving an invitation to play in an important game against a team from another part of the country—but we never watch the game or find out who wins. Ronny doesn't even appear in the last few pages. What's going on? What does "All-American" mean then, if we aren't going to see one?

As usual, it means that Tunis is toying with our habits of formulaic reading and thinking, especially about sports. And as usual, it means that our expectations, far from being fulfilled, will curtly turn on us. Like any good title—and any good book—*All-American* is full of surprises and ends up meaning a lot more than we expected. In fact, the words All-American do appear in the book, but not in a sports context. Ronny's father speaks them when he talks about the prep school boys' feelings of superiority:

"There aren't any peasants in this nation. There are just citizens, one as good as another and no better than the others, you and Goldman and Keith and all the rest of you. All Americans. Americans together, all of you." But because we expect the words only in a sports context, we fly right by them. Tunis is chuckling as we do.

As in Tunis's other novels, the athletic theme of the novel represents only one part—and a fairly superficial one—of the characters' lives. And as in his earlier books, Tunis darts back and forth from sports to tougher issues. In *All-American*, we find some of the old enemies of decent living (racism, capitalistic conservatism) and some new (snobbery, reverse snobbery, academic laziness), but as usual the challenge is met by defiant self-reliance, whereby young people take responsibility for the decency of a community by taking responsibility for themselves.

The drama comes from the tension between solitude and society, between individual conviction and group coercion. It begins with our hero Ronny leaving his excellent prep school because his teammates set themselves above "the peasants" at the rival public school. When he gets to the public high school, however, he's taunted as a preppy pretty boy and stands just as alone as before. Eventually he achieves assimilation, adjusting to different academic methods along the way (nobody supervises your study at a public school; you have to make yourself work). But just when he "belongs" the most—when he has led the football team to the threshhold of a postseason berth against a Miami high school—he takes a stand that isolates him once again. A black teammate is not invited to the game in Miami because of southern Jim Crow laws accepted unquestioningly by everyone at Ronny's northern high school—including the black kid. Ronny refuses to go and encourages the team to share in his boycott. The town's adult leaders, with fiscal investments in the contest, excoriate him for his foolhardy do-good stance; eventually, however, they agree to let the students of the school determine the course of action, by vote. Like *A City for Lincoln,* the book ends with a ballot.

Once again Tunis has beautifully integrated the elements of life into a sports story, managing to write about a star athlete without setting him above anyone. When Ronny changes schools and finds himself an outsider, when he falls in love, gets lazy, gets angry, or discovers that he has deep feelings about right and wrong that are not popular, his plight is compellingly common; we can identify with him the way we never can with a paragon. He is a good kid who sometimes messes up. Tunis never tries to make him a saint. Similarly, the other characters in the book resist our efforts to categorize them as Good or Bad; nearly everyone has moments as both hero and goat.

This is a major strength of Tunis's work. No author has been more deft at encouraging us to trust a character and then challenging that trust by allowing the character to make a mistake. The great thing is that we learn to stick with our affections without demanding that the people in the stories earn them by performing perfectly. We end up liking nearly everyone, too, despite their ups and downs.

This is not to say that Tunis is ambiguous about what is right and what is wrong. His sympathy for mistakes and his respect for personal initiative have their limits in works of fiction. As much as he insists on letting people make their own decisions, he does not let his characters get away with clever justifications that are only self-serving at the expense of the general progress of human nature and society. Even the most dedicated, compassionate, and pragmatic defender of (for example) racism could never win the day in a Tunis book. He is fairer than most writers to advocates of bogus causes; indeed, he often gives them a chance to have their say. The principal of the public high school in *All-American* is such a person. Tunis establishes him as a wise fellow of penetrating sensitivity, in his early conversations with Ronny. In the later chapters on the issue of the boycott, the principal—without suddenly sprouting fangs—presents a rational defense of racist practices. Tunis does not judge him for us; he doesn't use such writerly tricks as pejorative adjectives to lessen our regard for the guy. The author is as close to neutral as he could be; he lets us hear the presentation and judge for ourselves. Of course, it is nearly inevitable today that we will find racism to be wrongheaded. It was probably far less certain forty years ago that kids would reach the same conclusion. Nevertheless, Tunis left the kids to their own consciences.

Tunis knew a great secret about reading: When a reader reaches a conclusion on his or her own, the strength of that conclusion is directly proportional to the freedom felt in coming to it. A reader who simply receives the opinion of the author does not take it to heart. A reader who has to work to evaluate and choose *creates* something that goes beyond a lesson on the page. Again and again Tunis restrains himself from instructing and follows instead his principle of putting responsibility in the hands of the young. He treats his readers with exactly the same respect he shows for his characters. This, more than any explicit lesson he might purvey, demonstrates the truth of the premise on which all his stories are based: *We* know what is right, and when we are free we will follow what is good. That freedom is what America is all about—that freedom for all Americans.

—Bruce Brooks

All-American

1

Ronald stood waiting alone. He was the only player on the field you looked at, the only player you saw.

Feeling the tightness of the moment, the Academy stands rose together. Say, maybe this is it. Maybe this is the one we've been waiting for all afternoon. We can't let those meatballs hold us to a scoreless tie. That's terrible. That's the same as a licking. Maybe Ronny'll break through on this play. C'mon, Ronald old boy. Hey, hey, Ronny! Let's have a score.

On the field an official glanced at his watch. Only a few minutes left to go. Meanwhile across the gridiron the High School stands were in an uproar. Boy, have we bottled up that guy today! Sure, he's beaten us for two years; but he's stopped this afternoon all right. Only he's dangerous, he's still dangerous. Watch him, you birds; watch that Pretty Boy. Watch that fella, will ya? He's the one to watch. Watch him now, or he might break loose on this punt. One play and there goes the old ball game. Hey, Goldman! Hey, Stacey! Hey there, Fronzak! Watch that man! Watch that Pretty Boy, you guys!

Ronald stood waiting alone. While the High School went into their huddle, he balanced himself on one foot, clawed the dirt from his cleats, and then clawed at the other foot. Far up ahead the two lines leaned over the ball. The punt sailed up, up into the sky. A kind of expectant "Ah" came over the Academy stands as it settled into Ronald's arms.

Take out that end. Take out that end, someone. Shoot, why doesn't somebody take out Stacey. He's been in every play all afternoon. Oh . . . see that. D'ja see Ronny give him that straight arm! *He's off to town, he's off to town.* Go on,

Ronny . . . Ronny . . . Ronny . . . Aw! They've
got him by one foot. He's down.

From the stands you saw him; he was blotted
out by a mass of tacklers, while some player on
the ground held one shoe. He was almost down,
he was stopped, he was through. Suddenly without warning, as if by magic, he shot from that
mass of arms and legs and bodies and head-
guards and torn jerseys. He was free again.

Someone slapped at him and missed. Someone else grabbed out, caught his headguard and
ripped it off. His blonde hair shone in the autumn sunshine. He picked up speed, outraced
one open-mouthed, groping enemy at his elbow,
and reversing his field cut across in a kind of
sweeping S. The whole pattern on the grass dissolved into a number of units, all chasing one
man. Hands pawed at him, reached for him,
struck at his poised body, jumped at his head
and shoulders. He whirled completely around,
sidestepped a burly figure, slapped off another,
when someone jarred his body and upset his
stride.

The blonde head stumbled forward, the body
tripped and almost fell. His face was close to
the ground, yet his feet kept moving like pin-

wheels. Once again he appeared to be finished. But somehow he kept in motion, kept on running, stumbling, head down, until he managed to recover balance. His body control perfect, he swung back instinctively into open territory almost without raising his head.

From behind a huge shape came after him, fast, faster. Ronald glanced back, his mouth wide open in fatigue. Just ahead was the goal. He saw the pursuer gaining slowly. Now! Now then! The body came through the air and leaped for him. Ronald stepped deftly aside at the right moment. The tackler rolled over and over harmlessly on the turf.

Go on, Ronny! Go on, Ronny, go on, you Ronny-boy, only five yards, Ronald; go on, there he goes, he's over, oh, that Ronald, oh, that Ronny, that's for me.

Me, too.

II

On the scoreboard there was a 6 beside the word Academy. Visitors 0. An official on the sidelines glanced at his watch. He held up four fingers and Ronald saw them.

Time for them to score, the way Goldman was

moving. Plenty time for them to score. Four minutes to go. This was the moment when football was no fun. When you were all in and trying to protect a flimsy lead. Sort of like a bad dream in which you were chased by gangsters and couldn't run. It was all right at first. Oh, sure, at first it was all right, in the first quarter. Then you were fresh and keen and plays worked and there was satisfaction in the game. That was when football was fun.

You got tired and breathless in the second quarter and maybe knocked about a bit, but the half was ahead. The dressing room, with old Mike swabbing your face off, and the Doc taping your aching shoulder and fixing the cut on your leg, and Baldy patting you on the back and telling you how swell your interference was on Steve's runback.

In a few minutes, however, the agony recommenced. You hurt where Goldman had smacked you down at the end of that dash off tackle, time you were almost in the clear. Darn that clunk! And your bruised hip got stiff and tightened up under the pounding of the scrimmages, and you were sore where Stacey had banged into your injured shoulder. Your throwing shoulder. On purpose, of course! That's the kind of football they played, and your ankle pained where you'd yanked it away from LeRoy, their Negro end. Yes, you were just plain finished.

Then came that awful fourth quarter, and the score, and finally trying to protect the lead. When you were all in and wanted only one thing: to lie flat on the grass, to stretch out on that soft, warm turf. Yet you had to keep going. You had to keep thinking even though your head was dizzy, and at times everything spun round, and you were far too exhausted to call signals, and whenever the whistle blew between plays you realized your aching body and the need to sink down on your knees. When your lungs hurt so badly the only moment you could manage to forget the pain was in the excitement of play, lugging the ball yourself or carrying out some assignment. When your legs hurt all the way up, when your feet felt as if you were running in mud to your ankles, as if you were being chased by gangsters. By meatballs like Stacey and Goldman and Fronzak. Goldman's father, they said, used to be a bootlegger. Or a gangster, or something, anyway. Now he ran a clothing store at the corner of Main and State.

C'mon, gang! Mustn't let 'em beat us now.

Now we got 'em, these birds who expected to run away with us. Who thought we were a bunch of softies even if they were trimmed last year and the year before. Only four minutes to go! Four years to go. This is when you wished you'd never seen a football, when you hated it, all of it.

"Look out, Tony! Watch out for a pass. Hey, stop that man, stop Stacey! See, Tony, whad' I tell ya? C'm here, you guys. We got to get in and rush that passer. Keith, you and Rog and Harold rush him, will ya? Every play. That's the only way to stop a passing attack."

Across the field came the shrill-pitched yowlings of the High School cheering section. A girl in a white skirt and white sweater did a kind of handspring as Stacey brought the ball down to the 17-yard line, fighting and twisting and carrying Keith and Harold and Tommy Gilmore on his back. You had to hand it to that guy. He was a football player! So was Goldman. The shriekings increased as the pile unraveled. The girl cheerleader jumped up and down, irritating Ronald. Imagine having a girl cheerleader! Imagine girls in a school, anyhow. Then came the soothing, compact, full-throated roar. Ray . . . ray . . . ray . . . Academay . . . ray . . . ray . . . ray . . .

"Ok, guys! They can't score if only we stop Goldman and Stacey. Watch Goldman, Tony. Watch him and rush him every play. C'mon, gang, third and four. Here's our chance.

"*Look out*, Keith! He'll run, he won't pass, he'll run this time. He'll run, watch out. . . ."

The field dissolved again into a seemingly uncoordinated pattern. The big fellow with the cut on his face went back, his arm in the rear to pass. He drew in the two charging Academy ends, sidestepped one, dodged the other cleanly, and came toward an open space, picking up speed with every step. Ronald ran forward, the only player in his way. He feared he might miss the tackle through fatigue, so he threw himself at the burly figure and caught him on the hip. They went down together, on the 5-yard line.

"Nope. No, I'm ok. Wait a minute. Just my breath . . . that's all. Don't call time . . . we haven't more left. It's theirs? Ok." He sank to his knees. This was when you hated it, all of it. When you wished you'd never seen a football, ever.

The whistle blew. He raised himself slowly to his feet, while the others yanked on their helmets and leaned over in the huddle. Keith was talking. What's that? Keith never called signals, he was the captain. So you listened. "Let's take this bird Goldman. Let's get that clunk. Ronny, play up close. You hit him high, and I'll smack him low. Get me?"

The High School team came out of their huddle. Ronald could see them plainly now; big Fronzak, their tackle, his face red and bloody, and Stacey with one eye half closed, and Mancini, the other tackle, and in the backfield Goldman. The man to stop. The guy to get. He realized suddenly it wasn't football he hated after all. It was that bunch of mugs from town. No, it was Goldman.

There was the play. He found an opening and dashed in hard behind Keith. Goldman had the ball and was straightening up to feint. Ronny hurled himself at the extended chest and arm. Keith was diving for his feet at the same time. There was a crash, a snap, a cry of pain, and they all fell in a heap together. While a bobbling ball rolled on the grass beyond.

III

The autumn sun fell lower and lower until it dropped behind the chapel so that more than half the gridiron was in shadow. Beyond the crowded stands was the tower of the gymnasium, below on the side of the hill the line of red brick buildings which had stood there since before the Civil War. The Academy had tradition.

Faculty Row, with the white houses belonging to the Duke and the masters, was deserted. Spike, the Duke's airedale, who followed the boys from class to class, who was always waiting outside chapel for the Duke each morning, wandered alone and bored across the road. Main, which once had sheltered a member of Lincoln's cabinet as a student at the Academy, was empty. So was Belding, with its ancient iron cannon ball used in the old days to heat and curl up around for warmth in winter evenings. And Hargreaves where the Upper Formers all lived, and the old dining hall now used as a music department. Everything was a deserted village this afternoon.

You stood on Faculty Row looking off toward town and the smoking factories in the distance without seeing a single person. The scene, usually so alive with figures at that time, was a lonely one. For this was the day, the day when everyone woke up and said, "Looks like a good afternoon for the game, doesn't it?" The big day for the whole town. Big day for the Academy, too. The day of the High School game.

Shadows lengthened on the field. The Academy stands, yelling, standing, sitting, rising again, were noisy. The opposite side of the gridiron was silent. For once even the girl cheerleaders were quiet and motionless. Ronald went back to punt, wiping his hands on his trousers with that peculiar gesture of his. He extended his arms. A figure suddenly ran in front of his vision. The whistle blew.

The pattern of the field dissolved into a hundred, a thousand ants, vaguely running in all directions. The Academy band poured down and formed up behind the southern goalpost, while the boys invaded the grass, snatching each other's caps, pulling at coats, yelling, triumphant, shrieking the score. One-two-three-four-five-*six! six! six! six! six*! The players leaned over and gave a soundless cheer for each other, then stumbled across the tattered turf to the gymnasium. To the showers, to the voluptuous warmth and comfort of that healing spray, to the relief of the rubbing table. To rest at last.

In the gym the downstairs door opening on the field was open and bolted back. They poured through. Inside came the familiar sounds and smells: odors from the dressing rooms, the welcome hissing of the showers, the clack-clack, clackety-clack of cleats on concrete. To reach the stairs leading to their own lockers it was necessary for them to pass the quarters of the visiting team. These lockers were surrounded by steel netting rising up to the ceiling. There was a door in the netting kept locked when the team was on the field.

Now it was open, and the High School squad was wedging through. Funny what a difference victory made. You could tell by their attitude they'd been beaten. Just ahead of Ronny was Fronzak. He stumbled as he walked, and blood was oozing from a bad cut in the side of his head where he'd been kicked in scrimmage, and his head was slumped forward in fatigue. The headguard in his hand dropped to the floor but he didn't bother to pick it up. Back of Ronny was LeRoy. They always said if you kicked a Negro hard in the shins, he'd quit. Maybe. But that boy didn't, although his bare shins were all barked and raw. Ronny, despite his aches and pains, felt almost chipper compared to the High School team. Funny what a difference six points can make.

Then he lost his chipper feeling. Climbing the stairs, he glanced through the wire netting and saw on the concrete floor a recumbent figure in uniform. Half-naked bodies surrounded him, and two older men kneeled at his side. One man raised an arm of the figure on the floor. There was a sharp cry of anguish. Looking down, Ronald caught a glimpse of a face twisted in agony. Gosh! Goldman must be pretty bad. He must be hurt pretty bad. Why, we didn't mean to injure him. We only wanted to put him out of the play, that's all.

Their lockers were warm and smelly. Over everything were those welcome familiar smells, the smell of wet sweaty clothes tossed into a heap on the floor, of the ointments from the rubbing table, of the Iodex which Mike invariably used for sprains and bruises. Then there was the sound of running water from half a dozen showers going full blast simultaneously, and yells and shouts and noises from each one.

"Yee-ah, yee-ah, great going, guys. . . ."

"Nice work, Ronny. . . ."

"Ronny pulled us through all right."

"Oh, boy, I'll say! Yippee!"

"That last quarter, Ronald, when you . . ."

"Nice work, Keith . . ."

"Nice work yourself, Tony."

"I saw him set to pass so I . . ."

"Hi there, Ronny; say, were you hot . . ."

Only Ronald and Keith hardly spoke. They were both thinking the same thing. Why, we didn't intend to injure him. Honest we didn't. We only wanted to put him out of the play. That's football, isn't it? That's hard football, isn't it?

Funny how quickly you changed after a game. Ten minutes ago Ronald hated them all; the charging, rough Fronzak, the Negro boy who got hurt and kicked and wouldn't stay hurt, and Stacey at the other end who kept smacking him down whenever he tried to pass, and Goldman, that terror in their backfield all afternoon. Now he felt different. He didn't hate them anymore, especially since he'd noticed Fronzak's head droop and LeRoy's bloody ankles, and above all Goldman stretched out in agony on that concrete floor. Why, they hadn't even taken his uniform off yet. Nope, Ronald didn't hate them anymore. Not now. Football sure was a strange game. It did things to you.

He pulled off his soaking, stinking jersey, undid the straps to his shoulder pads, and yanked the cotton undershirt over his head. Through the steam covering the whole room he saw Baldy appear at the top of the stairs and stand there staring around. Usually Baldy was the first person Ronald wanted to talk to after a game. Baldwin Baldwin III, the old Princeton end, was a coach but he was more. He was the kind of man you liked to talk to even when you'd lost. Even when you'd pulled a bonehead play or fumbled a pass that meant the winning touchdown. What more could anyone say about a coach?

For Baldy had played football. He understood the agony of the last quarter. He always understood. Wonder, would he understand today? Somehow Ronny didn't want to talk to Baldy or anybody at that moment. He leaned over and yanked at the knots in his shoelaces. Why, we didn't mean to injure Goldman. Honest we didn't. We only tried to put him out of play. That's football, isn't it? That's hard football, isn't it?

In his deep heart Ronny knew this was untrue. All the time he kept saying the same thing over and over to himself. Gosh, I hope Goldman isn't hurt badly. If he's really hurt, I'll never play football again. Never.

IV

"Ronny." The coach sat down beside him on the bench. Ronald straightened up. "What really happened out there?"

"Gosh! Is he hurt badly, Mr. Baldwin? Is he hurt real bad?" He looked anxiously into the brown eyes of the coach. Then before he could stop himself the words poured out. "Why we didn't intend to injure Goldman, honest we didn't, Mr. Baldwin. We only wanted to put him out of the play."

Keith was standing over them. He broke in. "That's right. We just wanted to stop Goldman, Mr. Baldwin. We were only trying to stop that touchdown, any way we could. Is he hurt pretty bad?"

The coach stood up. "Yes, he's hurt. How badly we don't know yet. We hope it's nothing worse than a broken collarbone. They're afraid of a neck injury, but they aren't sure; they're taking him over to the Infirmary right now."

Ronald glanced across the room and saw the Duke, tall, commanding, erect. His overcoat was open and his hands clasped behind his back. He came toward the group, now encircled by half a dozen naked figures fresh from the showers, their bodies red, their hair all wet and glistening.

"How'd it happen, Baldy?"

"Why, Mr. Hetherington, it was one of those things, so far as I can see. The boys were trying hard to protect their lead, to stop Goldman and save a touchdown, and they caught him just right with their blocks. He was tired, y'know; when a player's tired he doesn't protect himself so well. That's when most injuries happen in football."

Did Baldy believe them? Had he seen it all from the bench? Had the play been clear from where he sat? Or was he trying to cover them up? All this Ronald thought as the Duke stood there looking down at him queerly.

The Duke glanced at Baldy, his hat pushed back on his wide forehead, perspiration showing from the heat of the steaming dressing room. Then he glanced back from the coach to Ronald sitting half-dressed on the bench, to Keith with a towel around his middle, to Tony leaning over his shoulder. Did the Duke believe them? Funny thing about the Duke; sometimes he didn't say much, but you seldom fooled him.

"I suppose you can't have football without injuries. But this is the first serious one we've had on the Hill for years. I'm sorry it had to happen here, like that, to a boy the type of Goldman, especially. They're taking him over to the Infirmary now and Mr. Curry, the principal, is with them. I think maybe we'd better get across and see how things stand."

He didn't congratulate them as he usually did, or tell them how well they'd played, or anything. Just turned and went out and down the iron staircase followed by Baldy. Maybe from his seat in the stands the Duke had seen exactly what happened. Hang it, we didn't mean to injure Goldman, honest we didn't. We were just trying to stop him, to put him out of the play. To save that touchdown. That's football, isn't it?

But all the time Ronald wanted to jump up and run after them. If only the other boys hadn't been there, sort of huddling around him, he would have leaped to his feet and shouted: It's our fault, Mr. Hetherington. We wanted to get Goldman. We were out to get him. They'd been roughing me all afternoon, Stacey and Goldman and that Negro end of theirs. They'd been playing dirty football. We were out to get him. Someone said, "You take him high and I'll take him low," and they carried him off the field on a stretcher. Like that. Maybe it was an accident. No, it was our fault. That's football. And if he's hurt, if he's badly hurt, I'll never play football again. Never!

That's what he wanted to jump up and shout. Instead he sat silently watching them disappear down the iron stairway which led to the basement and the visitors' lockers.

They always had dinner in the small room in Pierce Hall after the High School game, and when the speeches were over, and the Duke and Baldy had finished and made their usual jokes and given the same talk about what a fine thing the game was for the school and how at the Academy victory didn't really matter, that what counted was how you played; when that was all over they elected a captain for next season. Ronald had been in on three banquets. They were always the same.

That evening neither the Duke nor Baldy was there. They were over at the Infirmary waiting for the X-rays to be developed, while disquieting rumors came floating back to the squad sitting around the long table in the candlelight. Steve

Ketchum, who did some work in the laboratory of the Infirmary for his scholarship and knew his way around over there, reported that the doctors were afraid of paralysis. Or maybe something worse, he hinted. A specialist had been called from town and was due any minute.

Usually it was fun, a dinner after beating the High School. To beat the High School was something; anyone could whip University and those other teams, but the High School was something else. They might be meatballs but they sure could play football. So a victory over the High School was something. To whip that gang, who called us softies and liked to beat up an Academy boy if they caught him alone in their part of town, to lick that crowd who even laughed at us to our faces, that was really fun. When we won, the dinner was grand, and even the speeches afterward, Ronald felt, weren't hard to take. You had all the ice cream you wanted to eat when you really felt like eating it, too. When your bones had ceased aching so badly. When the throbbing of your nerves up and down your arm had died away, and you were warm and relaxed and happy in the candlelight around the table. Beside men you'd worked with all fall: Tony and

Keith and Rog Treadway and the others who'd pulled you through. Who'd opened up the holes. When you were with the team. Football was a team game, no matter what they said.

Not tonight it wasn't fun though. Not tonight. Tonight was different. For one thing, most of them weren't thinking about the dinner. They were thinking about that room in the hospital and Meyer Goldman, the High School halfback. Maybe he wasn't really hurt, maybe on the other hand he was. Maybe he'd die. Or would never walk again. His father kept a store on the corner of Main and State.

Gosh, we didn't intend to injure your son, honest we didn't, Mr. Goldman. We only wanted to stop him, to save a touchdown, that's all.

Ronald suggested that Steve be sent across to the Infirmary to nosey around and report. He was gone a long while, and when he returned everyone had eaten their ice cream in silence and finished seconds. There wasn't much conversation. Because there really wasn't much anyone could say. Nobody felt like talking over the game as they usually did whenever they won. No one felt like discussing football that evening, Ronald least of all. He was waiting for Steve to return. At last he came in, and his face, Ronald noticed as he entered the side door, was worried.

"They aren't sure yet, but they're afraid his neck is broken." The quiet in the room before was nothing to the silence now. It hung heavy over them.

"Then he'll die," someone said from the end of the table.

"Not necessarily. It depends, Miss Johnson the nurse told me. It seems the X-rays show he's got a broken clavicle vertebra. You can get well from that if you're careful, she says. After a long while."

Someone whistled, low, ominously.

"Of course it might not be, they aren't sure yet, but it's worse than just a broken collarbone; that's what they thought at first. Doctor Greene is there from town, and they're having a consultation now. What's that? Oh, a consultation is where the docs all get together and decide what they'd better do. His father's come up, so has his mother."

That settled things. Goldman's hurt. Goldman's really hurt. We did it, Keith and I did it; on purpose. If he's injured for life, I'll never play football again, never.

Now Keith was on his feet, talking.

Ronald hardly heard what he said, couldn't make out the words at first. He was seeing the Infirmary where he'd been laid up with flu the winter before, and the operating room where they took out Dave's appendix. He also saw Goldman's twisted face and his ugly mouth as they tore into him on that play.

". . . So I guess there's not much left now, you fellows . . ." Keith always called them "you fellows." . . . "There's nothing left 'cept the election of captain for next year. You all know this team is mostly juniors, only Dave Bradley and Stan . . . any nominations?"

Ordinarily there would have been some cracks and someone would have told him to reappoint himself and forget it. And Keith would have said solemnly, "Now look here, you fellows, we want a team that will do credit to the Academy and a man who'll lead them," and so on and so on. Not tonight. Everyone was serious enough without any urging. Tony stood up.

"There's one man I think we ought to nominate. He pulled us through against University School, he beat Country Day with three field goals, he was pretty near the whole team against Quaker Heights, and today, well, you all realize what he was out there this afternoon." He paused a moment. Then quickly, "I nominate Ronald Perry." And quickly sat down.

The first spontaneous expression of the evening swept the room. There was a chorus of approval all around the table. "Yeah, Ronny. Ronald Perry." Keith rose again.

"You just heard, you fellows. Ronald Perry's been nominated for captain. Anyone care to second it?"

"I do."

"Me."

"I do."

"Ok. Any other nominations?" Silence for just a few seconds. Then someone shouted from the end of the table.

"Move the nominations be closed."

"It's been moved and seconded that Ronald Perry be elected captain of next season's team."

"Wait a minute, please." Their faces were all sort of blurred below him in the candlelight, but he noticed them sit up suddenly. "Wait a minute. Guess you'll have to count me out. I can't take the captaincy of next year. I'm through."

"Through?"

"Through? You leaving school?"

"Nope. I'm just not playing football anymore."

2

Bong. Bong. Bong went the bell as the boys swarmed into chapel. At the Academy you had to wear a necktie to chapel and a necktie to dinner in the evening; otherwise you dressed as you pleased. They poured across the Quad from Main and Belding and Hargreaves. Lower Formers and Second Formers, Third Formers, Fourth Formers, and Upper Formers. A few of them wore black sweaters with the letter in orange on it, inside out as customary. Anyone who wore a varsity sweater right side out or front side to was looked on with disapproval at the Academy. He was said to be "chucking himself around."

It was a beautiful November morning, clear, crisp, and sunny. A few boys had turned the collars of their jackets up, others had put on fawn-colored polo coats, and everyone wore saddle shoes. Spike, the Duke's airedale, pranced along as he always did when he heard the chapel bell. Bong. Bong. Bong-bong. He paused beside one group, frisked across the grass of the Quad, bounced back and followed them gravely to the steps of the chapel, seating himself on the topmost step. His usual procedure.

The Academy had many customs. One custom was the foot-stamping after a football victory. Whenever the stars of the game entered chapel on the Monday morning, there would be a low stamping of feet. That day they stamped for Tony, they stamped for Rog, they stamped loudly for Keith. But news spread rapidly over the small world which was the Academy, and the news of Ronny's decision to give up football was news no more. When he came in there was a moment of hesitation. The stamp became a shuffle and then died away. The silent treatment. They were giving him the silent treatment.

Hey, Ronny's quit football! The boys whispered to one another. D'ja hear? He wouldn't take the captaincy for next season. Yeah, I know. That mean he isn't gonna play anymore? Guess so. He's upset. He says he's through.

The noise subsided as Ronny came down the aisle and took his seat in the second pew up front.

Usually the Duke made a kind of talk the morning after the High School game. He always found something to comment upon, and words of praise for the team, winning or losing. They waited, the whole school waited, wondering whether he'd mention the game or Goldman's injury. Goldman was hurt. So what? Football's tough. They thought we'd be a bunch of pushovers this year. They thought we were softies because we didn't play Madison High or Franklin High or teams from towns upstate. Because we preferred to play University School and Quaker Heights. Ok, now they found out. They got fooled. Served them right. As for Goldman, he happened to go down under a good block. Well, football's a tough game.

That's what the Academy thought while the opening hymn was being sung, and the Lesson for the day read and at last the Duke got up and stepped forward. As usual he had three or four slips of white paper in his hand. They were notices given him to read by different boys connected with school organizations. He adjusted his glasses.

"Candidates for the Monthly are requested to report to Gerald Staines in his room, 45 Hargreaves, this afternoon at five."

"Mr. Morrison wants the whole glee club to report at three sharp at Main. He says that means the whole club." Titters from the youngsters of the Lower Form in the balcony.

"The swimming team will begin practice at three this afternoon in the pool." Everyone sat up. The Academy had the best swimming team in the State, in fact anywhere in the region. Why, our men even made the Yale team, lots of them. No one could beat us at swimming.

The Duke continued. "Keith Davidson hopes . . ." there was a sudden insistent stamping of feet, and the Duke looked up quickly with a kind of frown on his face. "Keith Davidson, the captain, hopes for a good turnout. He wants new men to report, especially from the Second and Third Forms." His face turned down toward the last slip of paper in his hand.

"Found at the game, Saturday. Two fountain pens, one green, one black. Six notebooks . . . without any names in them." He lifted his eyebrows and looked at the school over his glasses. There were titters. Putting your name in your books was a fetish of the Duke's. Every year he mentioned it at the start of the term, insisted on everyone doing it, and every year a dozen boys forgot to do so. He waited a minute and then continued. "A silver cigarette case marked M. B." The entire school laughed openly. Smoking was strictly forbidden at the Academy. "If the boy whose father owns this case will call at Mr. Sullivan's office in the gym, he can have it." Now the school roared. That was the Duke's way of saying the boy wouldn't be punished. A grand guy, the Duke.

After a joke of this kind he usually became serious and gave them the works. They sat waiting for him to turn it on as only the Duke could. Today he stopped. Twisting his head, he made a sign to Mr. Morrison at the organ, and the school hymn began. There was a shuffle of feet while the boys stood and sang.

It was over. They swarmed into the aisles and

poured out the door. On the top step Spike was waiting, his tail going thump-thump against the wooden stairs. He stood up as Ronald appeared and greeted him by rubbing his face against his leg.

" 'Lo, Spike, Spike old boy." But all he saw was the row of smoking chimneys on the horizon and the distant roofs of the town where he would have to go in a few days.

He walked alone slowly across the Quad to Mr. Wendell's class in English. Just ahead was Keith's familiar figure, a regular halfback's physique, a short, thickset torso with his head built close to his body. You'd pick him out for a halfback anytime, anyplace. Keith went up the steps two at a time, jumping happily along. Things didn't seem to bother Keith. He never worried much. As he entered the room to the right on the first floor there was the stamping customary on the Monday following a big game when one of the stars entered the room. Ronny followed Keith and took his usual seat. No one made a sound. He understood; the silent treatment. Rex Heywood came in and sat down next to him. Then, seeing Ronald, he rose quietly and moved across the room.

Ordinarily this would have cut him. But he saw how they felt; to them he was a quitter. He was letting the school down. No one could appreciate it except maybe Keith and one or two members of the team. They could appreciate how he felt. Nope, even they couldn't. They just didn't feel the same way about it. Their attitude was different.

Because for the first time, he, Ronald Perry, had deliberately injured an opponent, put him in a plaster cast for life, or worse. In a few days he'd know definitely. After that, after what he'd been through since the game, he had no feelings left to be hurt by the school's disapproval. Now he was in another world, a world of bigger things than games and schools, a world of surgeons and casts and broken vertebrae, of life and even perhaps of death. He felt old, a million years older than his classmates around, familiar names and familiar faces he knew and liked. But occupied with winning or losing the High School game. To them Goldman was a clunk and his father kept a clothing store on the corner of Main and State, and what did it matter whether he was hurt or not?

That was their point of view. Ronald understood it, in fact he admitted to himself if he hadn't been the one to go in high on Goldman, it might very well have been his. When you had the responsibility of hitting a man high enough and hard enough to break his neck, or worse, you didn't care much about victory. You were in a different world. You suddenly became a man.

II

Keith would have gone, too, actually Keith offered to go. But Ronald wanted to go alone. He said he guessed he could represent the team all right. Keith didn't insist.

All the way down in the bus it came back to him; Goldman stretched out in pain on the concrete floor of the visitor's quarters in the basement of the gym. Suppose he was hurt for life. Once Ronald had seen a young man in a wheelchair who'd hurt his spine or something wrestling in college. Suppose Goldman was dead! Did they, could they arrest you for manslaughter in an accident of this kind? Manslaughter! An ugly word. His imagination pictured all sorts of things which could happen to Goldman.

At South Main he changed for a crosstown bus. As he came nearer and nearer the hospital he dreaded it more and more. He got out to walk the three blocks east, seeing the big hospital building ahead. For a second he wished he had Keith or someone of the team beside him. This going alone was not much fun.

It was like an office inside the dark interior. There was a window marked INFORMATION and behind it a girl at a switchboard, dressed all in white. She was busy pushing plugs into the switchboard, and it was some time before she yanked open a small wicket in the window.

"Whodjawannasee?"

"I'd like to see a boy named Meyer Goldman, please."

She paid no attention and continued putting plugs in and talking. "Orthopaedic. Doctor Thomas? Doctor Penny? His day off. Call Main, four one eight two. That's right. Orthopaedic. Orthopaedic Hospital. I'll ring him. I'm still ringing Doctor Thomas. I'll see if you can go up." This last to Ronald. "What's your name?"

"Perry. Ronald Perry." Maybe he wasn't allowed to see visitors at all. Must be pretty bad if he couldn't see any visitors. There was a conversation at the switchboard and she turned to him.

"Elevator at the right. Fourth floor. Room sixteen in the Dennison Ward."

He took the elevator and went up. This was the way you felt before the kickoff at a big game, before you actually got into it and lost your tenseness, before you got knocked around a little, and others got knocked around, too. The thought came back vividly of the man in the wheelchair, of Goldman stretched on the concrete floor, of Goldman in a wheelchair, a cripple for life.

"Fourth floor."

"Oh, yes, thanks."

A nurse was sitting at a small table. There was the same smell as in the dressing room after a game. Funny how everything went back to football.

"You're for Mr. Goldman? He can't talk much. And you aren't to stay long. But he wants to see you. This way, please." She preceded him down a wide hallway with doors at each side.

How is he? Will he live d'you think? Will he be a cripple, will he be in a chair all his life? Ronny wanted to question her, but he couldn't say a word, could only follow her down the hall. She threw open a door. "Visitor for you, Mr. Goldman."

On the bed was a figure. He didn't turn his head toward the door. The reason he didn't turn his head was because he couldn't. His whole neck was encased in a kind of ruff, a leather collar which came up clean around his chin. Beside the bed a man was standing. He stuck out his hand. The man was short, dark, and wore glasses. "Why, Mr. Perry, it's mighty good of you to come down here, hey, Meyer?" said Goldman's father.

Ronald hardly heard him. He saw only the boy in the bed and the collar around his neck.

" 'Lo, Goldman, h'are you?"

Ronald wanted to ask had he suffered much, was he going to live, would he have to wear that awful collar all his life, was he ever going to get well?

The lips above the awful collar moved; but Ronald could hear nothing.

One moment he was there, in the backfield, active, dangerous, threatening, the ball in his extended arm, a hated enemy. Then this. And I did it. Keith and I, we did it, we did it on purpose. We've maybe killed him, maybe we've broken his neck so he won't live. . . .

"Hullo, Perry." The voice was faint, the head didn't move, there was no expression in his face.

"Gee, Goldman, this is terrible . . . I . . . I mean the fellows . . . we all feel mighty . . ."

The man touched his arm and put his face close to Ronny's. His breath smelled of stale cigars. "After all, it's football. Football, ain't it?"

Despite his dislike of the man, a surge of warmth and relief swept over him. Then Goldman wouldn't die. He wouldn't maybe even be a cripple, even have to stay in a wheelchair. "You mean, you think, you hope he'll come out ok . . ."

"Sure! Why sure! Two months in here; as good as new. As good as new. He's tough; can't kill Meyer, hey, hey, can they, son?"

The face made some kind of an expression, still staring ahead.

"That's right, as good as new," said the older man.

"Say, I'm glad. We're all . . . we all feel pretty sick about this up at the Academy." Still the face was immobile, staring straight ahead.

It wasn't in the least what he had wanted to say, and the words sounded hollow and unconvincing. They *were* unconvincing. In his ears were the comments of the boys in Hargreaves, comments which hurt as he listened, which almost seemed to alienate him from the school. They were comments in tone and accent different from Mr. Goldman's. Aw, he had it coming to him, the big lug. He happened to go down under that block; so what? Football's a tough game.

But the older man kept on. "And the flowers. You never saw such flowers. The principal, that man . . ."

"Mr. Hetherington . . ."

"That's it. He came down with flowers, brought his wife, too. And the school sent 'em, and the team sent 'em. Please thank 'em for Meyer, and me, too. Please thank the gentlemen."

Somehow Ronald didn't feel at all like a gentleman. He felt uncomfortable and unhappy and anxious to get out. The face in that ugly collar staring straight ahead showed a sudden spasm of pain. Ronald broke away from the arm on his; as difficult as shaking off a tackler in a broken field. He approached the bed.

"Y'know, Goldman, I feel terribly about this.

About that block, I mean. Gee, I haven't been able to sleep . . . or do anything. You see we wanted to stop you, to save a touchdown . . ."

The face murmured something. He couldn't catch what it was, but the faintest kind of a smile came over the lips. "Ok." Or something of that sort.

If only they could see him, Ronald thought, if only they could see that awful collar up to his chin, and that set face staring straight ahead, motionless, expressionless. They wouldn't talk as they did. They couldn't.

"Guess I'll hafta be slipping along. Hope you get better, Goldman, and fast, too. The boys all wanted me to tell you how bad they felt about this thing." Once again, it wasn't in the least what he wanted to say. The things he wanted to say wouldn't come, and those he did say had no sincerity and no truth in them. What he wanted to say was:

Look; I can't sleep; I can't do my work; I can't hardly think about you; I can't talk to anyone at school; I can't discuss the thing at all, and when they mention your name and the accident it hurts me, inside, deep. Understand? I'm responsible, I did it. No matter what they tell you, it's on me; that's why you're wearing that awful leather collar, why your neck was broken. We did it on purpose, to put you out of the game. And we almost killed you.

No, it wouldn't come. Something stopped him. Instead he was saying, "So long, Goldman, I'll be seeing you." He backed toward the door, his forehead wet with perspiration, the man with the glasses still talking.

From the bed he could see that face without expression still staring straight ahead.

III

"Anyone heard how Goldman's coming along?" Half a dozen of them sat in Keith and Ronny's room in Hargreaves three weeks after the game.

"Dunno exactly. He'll be in the hospital quite some time before they let him out, I know. For further particulars, ask Ronny."

"Yes, Ronny probably knows. He's our authority on Goldman," remarked Tommy Gilmore.

"Ronny's practically a buddy of Goldman's these days; goes to the hospital all the time . . ."

"That's right," Keith interjected. "He goes

down about twice a week. Fact he's there right now."

"No, he isn't." Tommy was looking out the window. "He's coming across the Quad this minute."

There was a silence lasting some few seconds. Five of the six boys in the room were on the team, and they were thinking. Of the game, and Goldman's injury, and Ronny's refusal to play football anymore, and his strangeness toward them since. Almost as if he was an outsider. Someone remarked that Ronald seemed to be getting right fond of that Goldman lug, and then the moment's silence lengthened as his steps could be heard on the old wooden staircase.

"Hullo, men." His customary greeting. He glanced about the room, at the familiar faces; at Tommy with his legs drawn up as usual on the window seat; at Keith deep in the armchair before the fire; at Roger still carrying the scars on his forehead where he'd been kicked in a scrimmage in the High School game; at Eric Rodman, the big Number One back who could play any game at all and equally well, and to whom eight colleges had been talking, not knowing that he was going to Princeton as three generations of

Eric Rodmans had done before him. Ronald looked at them all, taking off his polo coat and muffler. All familiar faces, boys he had worked with, played with, fought with together in tough battles in different sports, friends. Yet strangers, too. Now at least they were strangers in a way. They were there, over on the other side of a river, and he was alone on the opposite bank, calling to them, and they didn't hear.

As he tossed his coat to the couch, they began their wisecracks to which he hardly listened.

"Where you been, Ronny? Slumming again this afternoon?"

"Ron's been out seeing how the other half lives," remarked Tommy from the window seat.

"How's the Duke of Plaza-Toro?" asked Eric. He was a great Gilbert and Sullivan fan, had a chest in his room with several hundred records, and always called Goldman by that name. Ronald came to.

"He's better. They think they'll let him out in two months. He's still . . . he still suffers a lot." Then despite himself it came out. He knew the moment he said the words it was foolish; he'd been saying it for several weeks with no effect. But still it crept out. "Gosh, I wish some of you men would drop in on him at the Orthopaedic some afternoon."

The silence came suddenly.

"Ok for you, Ronny, he's your pal."

"Nuts he's my pal. He isn't my pal at all. He's just a man I laid up in a football game."

"Yes, and I suppose two years ago, remember, when they laid out Johnny Staines and busted his leg, those meatballs came running up to the Infirmary to see him?"

"I don't remember. But . . ."

"Point is, Ronny," remarked Tommy in his southern drawl, "those lugs play dirty football; only when we get tough they don't like it. They expect us to play patty-cake 'cause we're from the Academy, and when we play just as hard as anyone . . ."

Ronny felt his face become hot. He was getting angry. He wanted to shout at them as loud as he could. Oh, sure. When *they* play rough it's dirty football; when *we* play rough we're just getting tough and playing hard.

Keith knew Ronald and saw his roommate's face redden. So he tried to change the subject.

"Football, football, don't we have enough football three months in the year?"

But Ronald was not to be hushed up. "I don't

know about dirty football but I bet that boy LeRoy is still limping from the bruises on his shins and legs."

"Yeah . . . but you know, Ronald . . ." Now Tommy was dispassionate and objective. He was even authoritative; he was talking about a subject which he knew. Of which they were totally ignorant. "You know, Ronny, they have no right to play Negroes on their team." He pronounced the word as if it were spelled Nigrows.

Ronald flared up. "Whad'ya mean they got no right? It's a free country, isn't it?"

"Oh, sure. It's a free country all right. Sure, they got a right, they got a right. Point is they hadn't oughta. Now down south we have separate schools and colleges for Negroes with their own teams and leagues and schedules and everything."

Ronald was stopped. He'd never heard of that. Nor had any of the others. They looked at Tommy on the window-seat with some interest.

"Certain. We give 'em their own teams and all, and they like it. Why, they'd much rather play with themselves."

"How do you know, Tommy?" Ronald was stung by the other's assurance.

"Oh, oh, I know. Down south we understand

how to treat Negroes. Up here, you-all spoil 'em." He paused. "Leastways, *we* think. Now we don't have any trouble; we love our Negroes. They're our friends, yes, sir. They are. . . ."

"Well, the way you got to LeRoy's shins and ankles that afternoon didn't look to me like you loved Negroes much, Tommy!"

The other sat up angrily. "Yeah. Ok! And I'll give him worse next year, too," he said with emphasis. "Him and that clunk, that boyfriend of yours, Goldman, and the rest of those lugs . . ."

"Me, too."

"Same here. When you're playing with a gang of thugs like that you can't be fancy. They think every year we're a bunch of softies; well, they found out this time."

"They found out—what?" Ronald was on his feet. Now he knew. He disliked them. Once they had been schoolmates, teammates, friends. Now they were there, over there, across that river, going away from him. He kept calling to them but they moved farther and farther away. "They found out—what? That we wanted to win the worst way, that what the Duke always said in chapel about playing the game was a lot of bees-wax, that all Baldy's talk about clean, hard football was tripe once we got on the field and saw we had a chance to trim 'em. They found out a lot of things. That we talked about sportsmanship but kicked LeRoy in the shins whenever we could, and ganged up on Goldman . . ."

"Yeah! What about them? Maybe they didn't all gang up on you whenever you tried to throw a pass?"

"Don't we call that rushing the passer?"

"And maybe they didn't go for your shoulder, that guy Stacey, their end. And Fronzak, always cracking Roger on his bum ankle in the scrimmages, and Mancini . . ."

"Why, those lugs, those meatballs," said Tommy, "they couldn't play clean if they tried. Those peasants . . ."

Inside Ronald something happened. For just a minute he was outside the whole world, he saw nothing in the room, lost the sound of voices all talking together in angry tones. He was entirely alone in a world with himself which nothing could penetrate. Then he heard his own words, cold hard words that came from deep within.

"Peasants! They're no more peasants than you guys."

"Yeah! You like 'em so darn well, Ronny,

looks like you'd quit the Academy and go down there—with your friends."

Ronald stood up. Now he knew exactly what he was saying. The red hot fury of anger suddenly passed. He was cool now, yet trembling. "You're quite wrong, all of you. They aren't my friends. They don't like me at all—yet. Maybe they never will. But you've got something there, Tommy; that's a good idea. I think I *will* quit this place. Right now."

His coat had slipped down to the floor from Keith's bed. Everyone was watching him wide-eyed as he slowly wrapped the muffler about his neck, his hand trembling in spite of all he could do to keep it steady. Taking one look around the room, he shoved on his coat. This room where he had been happy and was now unhappy. Tommy was right. There was no use staying on.

Down the hall his footsteps sounded. Then slowly on the wooden stairs. Inside, the room was dazed. Keith sat up straight, looking at Tommy and Eric, and Tommy looked back at Keith and Roger.

"Gosh!" said Keith.

"Aw . . . he'll cool off. He'll come back. You'll see, he'll come back by dinnertime. Just see if he doesn't."

"Aw, he's nuts," remarked Tommy. "Completely nuts, that's all. Been that way ever since he took that beating-up in the High School game. Why, he's been queer ever since then. I've noticed it." Tommy unraveled himself from the window seat, refusing to treat it as a major tragedy. What was the use of getting excited? Ronny would be back for dinner just as Eric said.

"Who wants to go over to the gym and shoot some squash?"

IV

"I don't know whether your father can see you this morning or not, Mr. Ronald. He's been in conference all morning with the board of the Terrington Company. I think maybe he has a luncheon engagement with them, too."

Miss Jessup in the outer office looked up at him. To break away from the Academy and people he had begun to dislike, who were beginning to dislike him, had seemed the natural thing to do back there in his room on the Hill. One hour later in a different and cooler mood, it appeared less simple. What would his father say? How would Dad take it? How would he like spending a thousand dollars to send him to the Academy and then find him walking out before Christmas? He always said, his father did, that it takes a long while to earn a thousand dollars.

Miss Jessup waited, sticking the end of a pencil into her hair, while he stood reflecting, saying nothing. "Hold on a minute. Take a seat and I'll just let him know you're here." She wrote his name on a piece of white paper and tiptoed into the inner office. Ronny could see her shoving the paper on the desk, and his dad's absentminded gesture, picking it up and talking to a man at his side all at the same time. The heavy odor of cigars came from the half-opened door. She returned. And gave him a gesture which said, maybe he'll come out and maybe he won't. Ronny waited.

In about a minute the door opened again and his father appeared. "Hullo there, Ronny. What seems to be the trouble?" There was a disturbed frown on his forehead, and Ronald realized he had probably come at the worst possible time. He should have considered that. Should have gone home and talked first of all to his mother. This he'd thought of doing, but was afraid she'd try to get him to go back. Besides, he's got to know sooner or later. It's impossible to return now. Well, here goes!

"Dad, I've quit school."

"Quit school! You mean you've left the Academy?"

Ronald nodded. There was a moment of silence. His father stood over him without a word, looking down hard, the frown deepening. Then he glanced quickly up, and looked at his wristwatch. "Ronny, I left my golf shoes over at Hanley's to be resoled. Here's two bucks; suppose you pop over and get them for me. Then meet me . . . meet me in . . . forty minutes. Meet me at the Crane and we'll have lunch, what say?"

"You bet, Dad, half an hour. That's a few minutes after one."

"Yes. Let's say one-fifteen to be sure."

"Ok." He was off.

Going down in the elevator Ronald felt lighter. There was a big load off his mind. Some fathers would have been sore. Some would have asked a lot of unpleasant personal questions there, right in the front office, before Miss Jessup and those other girls at the desks. Some would have exploded and talked about spending a thousand dollars for nothing, and made a scene. Not his dad, though. His dad took things like that in his stride. Still, Ronald knew he'd have plenty of explaining still to do. The ordeal wasn't over. It was hard work to make a thousand dollars, no matter what your dad did. The closer the luncheon came the less he looked forward to it.

"Now tell me all about it. Begin at the beginning." They were seated at a table in the big, cool grill of the Crane. Usually a lunch at the Crane was an event in Ronald's life. Not today.

"Dad, I hardly know where to begin. Where it all started, I mean."

"Well, what happened? Something must have happened to put you off like this."

"Gee, Dad." It was really hard to explain. Sure, he was a wonderful father. But suppose he didn't understand, didn't see things as Ronny saw them. Suppose he only thought about that thousand dollars, a thousand bucks; it took a long time to earn a thousand dollars.

"Well, let me ask you some questions. Marks bad?"

Ronny was annoyed. Why Dad knew better than that. "I should say not."

"Bust up someone's car?"

"Nosir."

"Girls?"

Ronald shook his head.

"Been smoking? Playing cards? Drinking? Coming in late at night? Breaking any rules?"

"Nosir."

"Well!" His father was stumped now. "Well, what on earth . . ."

"It's just, Dad, that I can't that I'm . . . Dad, I'm sick of them up there on the Hill." There it was. And probably his father would say, yes, you're sick of them but it's cost me one thousand dollars for you to find that out. . . .

"Oh! How come? Yes . . . the roast beef is mine. How come, Ronny? You always got on so well with the boys and the teachers and the Duke."

"You see, Dad, it started in that game. The High School game, remember? Remember when Goldman was busting our line into pieces there toward the end of the fourth quarter just after we'd scored our touchdown? Remember?" His father nodded. "Well, Keith said, he said, 'You take him high and I'll take him low.' An' I was tired, an' all in, an' trying to hold 'em, so . . . well, we went and did it. That's all."

"And broke Goldman's neck for him."

"Uhuh."

"H'm. I remember back in the Harvard game

of '16 . . ." Oh, migosh, was he going to tell that corny story about the Harvard halfback who scored a touchdown and was called back for holding in the line! No. Ronny with relief saw this was something else, something he had never heard before. Something his father evidently didn't talk about often. "Seems they had a top-chop quarterback; so our coach sent in a second string end at the kickoff, and during the first few minutes of play this end picked a fight with the Harvard quarter. A fist fight, right out in the open. Just by accident, y'understand. Well, of course they were both sent off the field. Harvard lost their best player and their mainspring. We lost a substitute end but the varsity end came right in so we were stronger than before. Get it?"

"I get it. That's the same idea, I guess. Say, Dad, weren't you a little sorry, afterward I mean, Dad?"

"Afterward, yes. In fact I've been sorry about that all my life. You see we won the game."

"Sure. So did we." After all, it was something to have a father who had played football, who understood these things. "I was sorry, too. Afterward. An', Dad, I kind of lied about it when they asked me . . . when they asked me, Baldy and the Duke an' all. I just said, I said, 'Why, we didn't mean to do it on purpose.' I said we just wanted to put Goldman out of the play. Keith and Rog and Eric said the same thing. Only they felt differently, somehow, Dad. They just said, 'Aw, he had it coming to him, the big lug.' Or the big clunk. An' I didn't; really I didn't. I felt if he was badly hurt, Dad, I never wanted to play football again, never. Never again."

"Oh. I see. I see lots of things. That's why you refused to take the captaincy."

"Uhuh. Seems like I never wanted to play anymore."

"Only the boys didn't understand, didn't agree with you; they didn't like it, did they? They thought you were letting the Academy down?"

"Yessir. I guess."

"Then what?"

"Well, Dad, then I went down to see Goldman at the hospital. He has to wear a terrible leather collar, all the time; it comes up to here, Dad. He can't move an inch. Gee, Dad, it's kind of terrible to see him and realize you did it all yourself, on purpose. That you might have killed him, or broken his neck for keeps if the blow had been an inch or two higher—or lower—or something. That you might have paralyzed him for life. So I wanted Keith and the other fellows to go down. Only, Dad, he's a Jew, and they said, 'Aw nuts, his dad used to be a gangster or something.' They wouldn't go."

Red crept over his father's forehead. "How ridiculous! His father's in the clothing business. I know him; he's no more a gangster than I am. He's made a lot of money, so have a good many others. Why, I know old man Goldman. Look here, who spreads these absurd stories anyway?"

"The boys, they said it. An', Dad, this morning I came back from the hospital; I'd been down to see him and he's in pain some of the time still. An' Keith and Rog and Eric were all in our room there, an', Dad, they said the High School plays dirty football, an' it made me mad after seeing him in that bed, so I said we do, too, an' then, I dunno, we got into an argument. Tommy got mad the first thing I knew, an' said, he said, 'Why, those peasants, they couldn't play clean football if they tried,' an' I said, 'They're no more peasants than you are.' . . ."

"What was that?" He laid down the cigar he was about to light. "What was that he called them?"

"Peasants. He meant Goldman and Stacey and Fronzak and that Negro end, LeRoy."

"Let me tell you something right here, Ronald." He lighted his cigar carefully but there was tremble on the end of the match. When he lighted a cigar that way and called him Ronald, that was bad news. Maybe he was going to talk now about the thousand dollars. It takes an awful long while to earn a thousand dollars. You can't waste a thousand dollars like this, son.

He began slowly. "First, let me say I'm sorry about all this. I wish you could finish out at the Academy. I want you to finish out at the Academy. You'll do much better at Yale if you come from the Academy. I don't even know whether you could get into Yale from the High School. Don't believe they send boys to Yale, do they? I don't want you to leave the Academy. But I understand your feelings. And I'm glad these things bother you. I'm glad you felt that way about breaking Goldman's neck deliberately."

"Y'know, Dad, I can't exactly say it, but something inside me, why, I just couldn't help that; I couldn't feel right with myself if I killed a man and kept on playing football. . . ."

"A poet once said it better a long, long while ago. 'To yourself be true.' That was the way he put it."

Why, of course. A new world suddenly opened

up to Ronald. Mr. Wendell, the English master, had often quoted them that line. Then it meant nothing, words, a verse, a line of poetry. Something written somewhere, sometime, by some famous old geezer. Poets didn't have any relation to life; they were just something you had to read during the nine o'clock study period in Hall. Now the whole thing came home. Now he saw poets had something to do with school after all, something to do with life, with him, with Ronald Perry. He realized more clearly why he felt as he did. Yet all he could do was mumble, "Uhuh."

"I don't blame you for seeing red, for feeling the way you did. Calling names like peasants and clunks and all that is no good. It's no good in the United States. There aren't any peasants in this nation. There are just citizens, one as good as another and no better than the others, you and Goldman and Keith and all the rest of you. All Americans. Americans together, all of you."

"Yeah, an' he said, Dad . . . I mean that's what I said. What I tried to say, only I couldn't say it like you do. I got mad and said, 'They're no more peasants than you guys'; and Tommy said, 'Ok. You like 'em so darn well, wonder you don't quit the Academy and go down there with your friends in the High School.' So I said, 'They aren't my friends. They don't like me.' Know what they call me down there, Dad? They call me . . . Pretty Boy. Because I got yellow hair. Pretty Boy Perry. I know. I heard. But I said to Tommy, 'Ok, they aren't my friends; but I think I *will* quit the Academy, quit right now.' So that's why I'm here."

His father was watching closely, saying nothing. The cigar in his hand had gone out. Ronald couldn't tell quite what his dad's feelings really were, what he felt about it all, whether he was still angry or whether he was beginning to think of that thousand dollars. Because his father kept silent, the cigar smokeless in his hand, all the time looking at him hard.

"Well, Ronny, I'll say this much." He relighted the cigar. "I'll say this; I'm sorry you acted so impulsively in a way. I wish you'd acted more deliberately. But then again, I don't know, I'm not sure; I suppose at your age I'd have done the same thing. I can't say you came off second best, either. Now let's do this. We'll go home. We'll think it over and talk it over together during the weekend. If you still feel on Monday morning you want to leave the Academy and go to the High School, it's fine with me."

Not a word about the thousand dollars. Not a single word about the money or how long it took to earn it or anything. Nothing but that.

Which is how Ronald (Pretty Boy) Perry, the star halfback of the football team, who pulled them through against the University School, who beat Country Day with three field goals, who was the whole darn team against Quaker Heights, that's how Ronald Perry happened to leave the Academy in the middle of the term to go to Abraham Lincoln High.

3

So this was Abraham Lincoln High!
Ronald sat on the long bench in the outer room waiting for the principal to see him. Behind a counter three girls were whacking away at typewriters. A fourth leaned over the counter talking to a student. The place was an office, a business office. Not at all like the Duke's study where he received you on the Hill.

The Duke's big room was attached to the rear of his house. You entered to find yourself in the midst of a library with books on shelves reaching clean up to the ceiling. The room was paneled in pine; on one side between the windows a log fire was burning, opposite was a deep leather couch. *Time*, *Life*, and other magazines were always heaped up on the tables or lying on the floor where the Duke had dropped them. Often he would be found standing before the fire, legs apart, sucking on an unlighted pipe. There was, to be sure, a small office adjoining this room where there was a desk with a telephone on it; but the Duke invariably received you in his book-lined library.

Ronald sat waiting. The moment had come. It was like going to the dentist and waiting outside. And it was going to hurt like the dentist, in another way. The one thing he couldn't do was talk about the accident, about Goldman, about how it happened. With his father, yes, but with no one else. And these were the questions he would certainly be asked.

With a sigh he picked up the *Mercury*, the school paper, from a table beside his seat. There was a tabulation of orchestra popularity, and he ran his eye down the column.

1. Glenn Miller 1,256
2. Tommy Dorsey 1,165

3. Harry James 1,000
4. Jimmy Dorsey 914
5. Vaughn Monroe 907
6. Sammy Kaye 842
7. Benny Goodman 769
8. Artie Shaw 533
9. Johnny Long 412
10. Count Basie 388

When he got that far, someone came hurrying past. It was the principal who went into his room and shut the door. One of the girls jumped up from her typewriter and followed him. In a few minutes she came out. "Mr. Curry'll see you now." She looked at him curiously as he went in to the dentist's chair.

Certainly this man wasn't a personality like the Duke. That was Ronald's first impression. The Duke was big and tall; sort of man made you wonder who he was if you met him on the street. No one would ever wonder about Mr. Curry. You'd just never see him. You'd walk right past. No one would ever guess he was the headmaster—that is, the principal—of a big high school like Abraham Lincoln.

"Ronald Perry? How d'you do. Mighty glad to have you with us, Ronald." Ronald mumbled something. He disliked people who called him Ronald the first time they saw him. Somehow this wasn't working out quite as he'd expected.

Mr. Curry began asking questions, the usual sort of questions. Ronald replied eagerly.

If only he won't ask about the game, if only he won't talk about Goldman and the injury.

In a dry monotone he inquired whether Ronald was going to college. To Yale. H'm . . . taking fourth term work . . . h'm . . . that would correspond to the junior class, pretty much . . . h'm . . . let me see, you're eighteen . . . no, seventeen, yes, the junior class . . . that would be about right for you as a junior, wouldn't it?

Ronald thought that it would. Yes, he'd be a junior.

The principal continued, talking still in the same undertone. Ronald looked at him, at his glasses, at his clothes. Nothing at all distinctive about the man. When he spoke he seldom looked at you. Always he seemed to be glancing out of the window, at the wall, at the ruler in his hands—anywhere except at his caller. The Duke looked directly at you. The Duke sat you in that red leather couch and stood with his hands behind his back in front of the fire, fixing you with his eyes. If you were sent over by one of the masters you could be sure of a bad half hour. Somehow you couldn't feel that way about this man, the way you felt about the Duke. The Duke, as Ronald was more and more realizing, was a personality. Mr. Curry was not.

He pushed a button. The girl appeared. She looked curiously at Ronald again.

"Get Jim Stacey." Then to him, "You must know Jim. Played end on our team last fall."

Here it comes! He held on to the chair. Here it comes. What'll I do! What'll I say!

But the principal went on without a pause. "He'll show you around the school and introduce you to your teachers. You'll be in Mr. Kates' room."

Gosh! Isn't he going to talk about it? Isn't he really going to mention the injury, or Goldman, or anything? Maybe he won't. Maybe he isn't going to talk about it. His respect for the quiet man in the glasses rose quickly. Then Stacey entered.

His red hair was all on end, his freckled face was grinning. He was not in the least disturbed by being called to the office of the principal. He shook hands with Ronald, his smile widening as he listened.

"Yessir. Sure. Yessir." He knew. He understood. The principal called him Jim and not Stacey. It seemed strange to Ronald for all the teachers at the Academy called you by your last name.

The principal shook hands and wished him luck. Ronald mumbled something, and together they left the room and went into the hall. The wide corridors had murals on each side; scenes of sport—baseball and football and basketball. Stacey said nothing. Ronny said nothing. Presently his guide broke the silence.

"You gonna come here? To school?" Ronny felt immensely alone and unsure of himself in that strange place. There was a sort of defiant sound in the other boy's tone.

"Yeah, I guess so."

"Oh."

Not exactly a cordial welcome and he'd hardly expected a cordial welcome. Why should they be cordial? Then before anything more could be said, a bell rang, they were in the corridor and caught up in a noisy mob of boys and girls.

Everything was so different. It was all different, even the school building was different from what you saw on the outside. Naturally he knew things would be different; but not as different as they were.

The Academy had tradition. Hargreaves and Main and Belding were old and familiar and warm, with thick ivy vines climbing up their stone walls. Inside, the floors were scuffed; so were the battered doorsills, and each building had the accumulated odors of generations of boys who had lived there. They gave, even to a stranger, a kind of friendly homeliness.

Abraham Lincoln had nothing of the sort. It was all different. For one thing, it was modern and impersonal. Its bricks were fresh, not old and faded by age, and the trim around the windows was clean white stone, not carved and battered white woodwork. Instead of being scuffed and worn, the floors were large tiles of gray and black. The whole building was as warm and friendly as an ice cream factory. Carried along by that noisy human tide down the hallway, he suddenly remembered one of the masters at the Academy referring to Abraham Lincoln as an "educational factory." That phrase meant something now.

Stacey stopped before one of the lockers that lined the hallway and showed him the combination: 8. 17. 9. He tried it himself, opened it with Stacey silently watching, and shoved his coat inside. Then they went down the hall to Mr. Kates' room. The teacher, evidently expecting him, came forward. All the faces in the room turned together toward the door. There was an undercurrent of titters from desk to desk. He could swear he heard the words "Pretty Boy" several times. One or two girls recognized him and began giggling to each other. With some repulsion Ronald realized that girls were like that; they were always giggling.

Mr. Kates was short, pleasant, unassuming, like the principal. It was a study period, so he sat down with Ronald in the rear of the room and discussed his work at some length. In Abraham Lincoln you didn't sit at an ancient desk with dozens of names like "Chandler, '22," or "Royce, '34," or "Farnsworth, '29" carved so deeply in the grimy wood you could hardly write on it. You sat here in a kind of combination seat and desk connected with metal tubing. The whole affair was new, clean, and practically unbreakable. Moreover the desks were of varnished hardwood that discouraged attention. Ronald felt the smooth, rigid surface.

Then a bell rang somewhere. The whole class rose together, dumping their books into piles. Stacey led him down the teeming corridors, and they passed several boys whom he recognized as football players. Along came a black-faced pirate; it was a black face; it was a pirate. Ronald, as they drew near, saw it was Ned LeRoy dressed as a pirate with a sword at his belt. He paid no attention to anyone and nobody paid attention to him.

"National Thespians," explained Stacey. "See, he's being taken into the National Thespians, the dramatic society. He stole the show in our school play last week."

The next class had a woman teacher. It was Ronald's first woman teacher, and he had a prejudice against women teachers. This also was his first real class, and he looked around. It was a large class compared to those at the Academy, two or three times as large; about thirty-five in all, including many girls. Every other girl wore a sweater. There were yellow sweaters, white sweaters, blue sweaters, red and pink sweaters, many pink sweaters. The boys wore varsity sweaters with the letters plainly visible outside, yet no one seemed to realize they were chucking their weight around. Some had on windbreakers, a few wore no coats at all. Almost nobody bothered with a necktie.

What struck him most was the different discipline. Even in Mr. Wendell's class, which was known for its informality throughout the Academy, the class discipline was much stricter. While the teacher distributed some corrected papers, there was a steady hum of talk and conversation. She looked up and stopped. "Shsss . . . not *quite* so much noise, please. . . ." Ronald smiled to himself, thinking how the masters at the Academy would have immediately handed out detentions.

The papers were finally distributed and she called on the class for book reports. "Gordon Brewster."

A small, black-haired, olive-skinned boy, slender and rather good-looking, walked to the front of the room. With assurance he began an account of a book he had read. It was done, to Ronald's amazement, more smoothly and better than many boys could have done on the Hill. But Stacey's head with the bristling red hair kept wagging in disapproval. His hand shot up. The teacher saw it but paid no attention. Stacey made it evident that he didn't like the boy who was reciting. Finally he could restrain himself no longer and interrupted.

"Naw . . . he's wrong, Miss Davis, he's wrong on that date. 1862."

She was cool, sharp, efficient in her tone. "I'm sorry, Jim; he's right. It was 1864."

The snub didn't affect Stacey in the least. He continued to make derisive noises, apparently doing his best to upset Gordon Brewster who refused to be upset. This continued until the bell rang and the class, taking no notice of the boy reciting, cut off his last sentences in a Niagara of noise. Gathering their belongings, most of the boys and girls turned their backs on him and tramped out.

From every room crowds poured into the wide, cool corridors, filling them completely. The sound was terrific; the strangeness of it all, the uproar and confusion, dazed him. It was like being lost in a big city; so many unfamiliar faces, so much rush and bustle and turmoil on every side, that he was completely unsettled.

Then he heard a sound. A sound which pulled

him from the deep well of his bewilderment, which yanked him back to that hallway. It was a voice from behind in the milling mob, a boy's voice, high-pitched, imitating a girl. It was calling in derision.

"Oh, Ronny! Oh, Pretty Boy . . . !"

II

Class followed class. His head was dizzy with the confusion and largeness of the place. Shortly after twelve he tagged along with Stacey to the cafeteria on the third floor, for luncheon.

The cafeteria was an enormous room running the whole length of the building, with what seemed like hundreds of tables in rows. Around the walls were more oil paintings. Opposite the doorway was the cafeteria itself. You entered, took a tray from the counter, put on it whatever you wished from the menu, and then paid as you went out. Ronald chose scrambled eggs, potato chips, a piece of pie, a bottle of milk, bread and butter. Cost: 27 cents.

They emerged from the cafeteria proper to the main dining room, or at least he did, and stood holding his tray and feeling awkward. It seemed as if a million girls sitting at the tables were watching. After a minute Stacey joined him, holding out silverware.

"You forgot yer tools."

"Oh, thanks." They found an empty table and sat down on the aisle, Ronny opposite the other boy. Stacey ate rapidly and in complete silence, although judging from the noise around them he was the only silent person in the entire room. As Ronny ate his scrambled eggs, he looked about.

To his surprise he saw that those paintings on the four walls were actually scenes of life in and around the town. Not mythological Greece, or ancient history; but the town itself, today. There were scenes of people eating lunch in Forest Grove, or swimming in the Lake, or skiing in the hills up back of Jamestown. As he ate, looking at the paintings on the walls, he became aware of the same high-pitched giggling he had heard in the corridors. Girls with heads together at different tables were glancing his way. Across the aisle he saw Fronzak the big tackle. He hoped he'd look up and smile; but he didn't. Ned LeRoy was eating at a table in one corner with half a dozen colored boys. The table next to them was half-filled with colored girls. Ronny observed that most of them were eating out of paper bags containing lunches brought from home, not off trays purchased at the cafeteria as did nearly everyone else.

Then he realized that his conductor had finished and was leaning back in his chair. No one wastes much time eating in this place, he thought.

"You take yer tray and hand it in at that window back there by the door, on the way out." Stacey indicated the window over his shoulder, and Ronald noticed boys and girls already passing by with their empty trays. He finished his pie and gulped his milk. Grabbing the tray, he rose hurriedly just as Stacey, across the table, was getting ready to rise also. Clumsily he hit the Irishman's foot, stumbled a little, not much but enough.

CLASH! BANG! CLATTER! There they were— tray, dishes, silverware in a mess on the floor.

Before the noise had died away a roar started. Gently at first, then louder, louder still. All over the room in unison six hundred and fifty throats opened wide.

He stood dazed by the sound. It was terrifying. Every eye in the room was on him. Never in his life, not even out there alone in the backfield on the Academy gridiron, had he felt so conspicuous. And so helpless. The roar continued. It grew. Red and flushed he leaned over to scoop up the remains of his luncheon.

Then down the aisle holding the fragments of disaster in his hand. It seemed a million miles long, that aisle. Gosh, what a dope I am! What a way to begin a school! How could I come to make such a fool of myself!

The aisle was endless. Finally he reached the window. Stacey was there beside the pile of trays and dirty dishes with a kind of malicious grin on his face. Shoving his burden beside the others, Ronald turned and went into the corridor with his red-haired companion. Behind them the roar was slowly dying away.

"Yeah . . . they always do that when you smash or drop something. It's a custom here." The boys and girls passing by grinned widely, and Ronald, still red and angry with himself, hardly heard Stacey's comments as they went downstairs.

"See that guy, see him? He's Mr. Morgan, physical ed. You hafta take it twice a week if you aren't on the varsity. This here's the liberry. This is the music room. We've got the best high school band in the country."

Oh, you have, have you? thought Ronald,

vaguely remembering the band from the day of the game. He was still too annoyed with himself to talk, and through the next class, an advanced algebra course, he felt hot and conspicuous all the time. Luckily this class was attended by fewer girls than boys. In fact there were only two girls in it. Evidently girls disliked algebra as much as he did.

Discipline here was stricter, attention better, although he saw that nearly everyone still kept an eye on the clock in the rear of the room, something never tolerated by the masters at the Academy. He himself had to follow closely, and he liked the teacher, a quick, active, elderly man who seemed to know his stuff. This man made the boys recite. They got away with nothing. "I don't think the others can hear you," he remarked to a pupil who was mumbling the lesson.

Then followed a Latin class with a woman teacher, and before he knew it the final bell rang. He was tired, dead tired. The noise and confusion and especially the newness of it all were wearying.

With Stacey he went upstairs. Already lots of the kids were pouring down, the girls carrying books home to study. Ronald noticed that few of the boys had books under their arms. He grabbed his coat from the hook in the locker.

"Well, s'long. I'm gonna try out for the swimming team. You can't swim, y'know."

Ronny slammed his locker shut. Two or three hundred lockers up and down the long corridor were being slammed at the same time and the noise was overpowering.

"Oh! Why not?"

Stacey had to shout over the sound of banging lockers and yelling boys and girls. "Ten weeks rule. No transfers can play varsity athletics 'cept after ten weeks." Was there a trace of satisfaction in his tone? "S'long. See you tomorrow." He turned away and was lost in the crowd.

Tired, confused, still annoyed with himself, Ronald went down the stairs alone in the chattering crowd. Every one of these hundreds of boys and girls knew each other, called each other by first names, yelled at each other. Everyone was either with a group or some one kid. The girls each had an arm in another girl's, the boys were joking to a pal as they rushed down the long hallways. Ronny felt almost homesick for Keith and Rog and the boys with whom he had fought at the Academy.

There was a sort of jam at the main doorway. He stood aside watching them swarm through. Then he came out with the crowd into the sunlight. Cars were lined up at the curb; at one side was the long bicycle rack with double rows of bikes awaiting their owners. Then from behind, from inside the door, he heard it, now distinctly.

"Oh, Ronny! Oh, Ronny!" It was a boy's voice, high-pitched, imitating a girl. Or trying to.

Ronald went down the steps. Somehow this wasn't working out quite as he'd expected.

III

On the bed was the boy in the leather collar, looking straight ahead, and in the chair at the foot of the bed was the boy who had helped put him there.

"How do I know? Oh, I do, that's all."

"But, Meyer, *how* do you know?"

"Well, I'll tell you, Ronald. I know 'cause I've been there."

Ronny was amazed. "You have! Really! You went to the Academy, to some school . . ."

"Nope. You don't get me. I mean I've been where you are now. I've been in your place."

"In my place!"

"Uhuh. Y'see, Ronald, it's like this. A Jewish boy, now, he's behind the 8-ball all the time. It isn't enough to be better than the other guy, he's gotta be a whole lot better."

"Has he? How you mean, Meyer?"

"Well, I mean like this. Is he after a job, he's gotta be twice as smart as the other boy, else he don't land that job. Get me?"

Ronald got him.

"Like, now, is he trying to get a scholarship to college. His marks must be lots higher than the other boy or the boy grabs off the dough. See?"

Ronald saw. The other boy. Why, that's me! That's Keith! That's Tommy Gilmore. It's some of the kids in Abraham Lincoln, even. Ronald saw. What he saw he did not like.

"Well, yes, I suppose you're right."

"Now me, for instance. I want to be a doctor. I want to, understand. I'm set. My old man says sure, he'll help me. He'll give me dough. I get my marks; I'm set. Will I get into Medical School? Maybe so, maybe not."

"Why not, Meyer?"

"Why not! 'Cause I'm Jewish. Lots of the Medical Schools don't want me. They don't say so, out loud, that is. But they don't and I know they don't." His face looking straight ahead was stern.

Ronald felt uncomfortable as that determined voice continued. This was something he'd never before realized. When you were on the Hill, you thought of the kids at Abraham Lincoln as meatballs, not as boys trying to get into Medical School. On the Hill boys were going to Medical School, only they took it sort of for granted. Eric Rodman, for instance. His old man was a doctor and lived in New York. Once Ronald had stayed with him during vacation, and they went to shows, real shows not movies. And when they got home Eric's old man was there. Eric would get to Medical School, he would get to be a doctor.

It was hard. But anyhow, there was one place things were pretty ok. He blurted out what he felt. "Only not in sport, Meyer; it isn't that way in sport."

To this remark the stiff-necked figure on the bed would have to agree. But there was a moment's silence. "Sometimes yes, sometimes not. D'you ever hear of a Jewish boy on the crew at a big college? Nope. It's like a Negro in the big leagues."

Wait a minute. Hold on now. This was too

much for Ronald. "You mean to say if Ned LeRoy was a . . . was a great first baseman like, well, like Hank Greenberg, he couldn't make the Tigers?"

He laughed, not a happy laugh either. "Why, no; 'course not, Ronald. Name me one Negro ballplayer, one."

"H'm, now, that pitcher, that one, you know . . ."

"Satchel Paige. Sure. He's maybe the best pitcher in all baseball. Only he isn't in the big leagues. Say! Do you know what league he's in? I'll tell you. He's in our league. And now you're in our league, too, and you don't like it. You don't even understand it the way we do because we were brought up in this league. We're on to their curves."

"Whose curves?"

"The other guys." There was hardness in his voice. "The guys who get the jobs, the scholarships, the places on the Yale crew and the Tigers."

This wasn't so good. He was going to Yale. Say, was that true? Was Yale like that? Were the rest of the colleges that sort of places? Gosh. Made you sort of think, all this Meyer was saying.

He looked at the figure stretched on the bed. That's where he'll be tonight when I'm doing my French and Latin in my own room, and tomorrow when I'm trying not to hear them in the hallways, and the next day, and the next. This is the guy they called a meatball, this is the boy they ganged up on. We ganged up on. There he is, lying with a queer leather collar up around his neck and a pained look in his eyes.

It made him angry all of a sudden. "But look here, Meyer, what do you do?" This was unjust. It was unfair. That Meyer couldn't get a scholarship if he earned it, that Ned could never play first for the Detroit Tigers. Gosh, it was wrong, all wrong.

"What do we do? We don't do anything. We learn to take it. That's why you're in our league now, Ronald, and that's what you've got to do, learn to take it."

Thank goodness he didn't add, "and like it." No one in his senses could do that. Meyer was right. At the Academy he hadn't taken it; he hadn't taken the silent treatment, the unfriendliness, and all the rest. He'd gotten up and walked out. Now he had to learn to take it.

Only if there was all this unfairness, all this injustice, why did older folks like teachers and the principal and the Duke talk about America? And democracy. And all that sort of thing. Why did they? Why?

"Look, Ronny, since this . . . since that game . . . since I got to seeing you so often, I can tell you things you maybe don't know. Now take that trick Stacey pulled on you in the cafeteria the other day . . ."

"What! You mean to say he did that on purpose!" It was the kind of thing which could never happen in the Academy. Nobody there would think of humiliating another boy before the school. He saw suddenly that not all the meanness and cruelty was in the Academy, that it was here, too, right around him, a different kind perhaps; but there it was.

They looked at each other; the boy in bed amused, for the first time a sort of smile on the lips above the leather collar. And sitting at the foot the boy who had helped put him there, shocked and worried.

"Why, sure he did. But look, he's a good guy, Stacey is. Yes, really. Only he thinks you aren't one of us, understand. At heart he's an ok guy."

"Takes a funny way to show it," remarked Ronald.

"Sure. That's Stacey. He'll ride you, but give

him time. He's not a bad guy. I know. He likes to make folks think he's tough."

"Oh! Is that his trouble?"

"Yeah. Now you're in the same situation I was. He'll ride you plenty, all he can. Tried to pull that stuff on me, and finally I told him, I said, 'Looka here, Stacey, lay off me or I'll poke you in the puss.' I'm bigger'n he is, so he quit. Then we became friends, good friends, too. So'll you."

"Maybe." Ronald in his distress doubted it.

"Of course. Only you mustn't let him get away with anything. Call him sometime and he'll quit. He's ok; I know you mightn't think so after what he did up in that cafeteria, but he's a good guy, honest he is. He thinks right, get me? Understand?"

In a way he did understand. It was hard to believe about a boy who'd stick his foot out in the cafeteria on a stranger; it was hard to believe about that fresh kid with straight red hair and the freckles and the queer clothes. But if he thought right, after all, that was what counted. Ronald felt he could trust Meyer Goldman. If Goldman said so, it must be so. Besides, many of them like Keith and Tommy wore the right clothes, shirts with collars that buttoned down and saddle shoes, only they didn't think right. They were nice guys, but they didn't think right. That was what counted, and if Goldman said so, it must be so.

He went down the steps to the street, thinking hard. The picture ahead was not attractive. Ronald hated fights, scraps, brawls, especially when people were around. Well, I'm in their league now, Meyer's and Ned LeRoy's.

For the first time since arriving at Abraham Lincoln High he saw the funny side of the thing. You were the best back on the Academy team, and you ended up in the league with Meyer Goldman and Ned LeRoy. This he had hardly expected that morning up in Keith's room on the Hill when he'd exploded out of Hargreaves, out of the Academy, out of everything he was used to and into a very different league.

IV

Stacey leaned toward him. "Hey, Ronald, lemme have a look at your French paper, will ya?"

Ronald glanced up, uneasy. Mr. Robinson,

the history teacher, was handing out corrected papers, with his back turned. So Ronny slipped his French lesson across, feeling uncomfortable. At the Academy this was never done, first because the teachers would catch you, second because they were there for help day and night, and third because as a rule every boy came to the first period prepared. At Abraham Lincoln as a rule almost every boy came to the first period unprepared.

Mr. Robinson came down the aisle toward him, handing out papers and calling names. "Gracie . . . John . . . Rosie . . . Bob . . . Sue . . . Paul . . . Barbara . . . Susie . . . Donald."

The first names jarred on Ronny's ears. At the Academy the masters called you by your last name: Perry, Davidson, Treadway, Rodman. Most teachers at Abraham Lincoln called you by your first name. He much preferred the Academy method.

Hang it, he always preferred the Academy method; he wished he didn't but he did. Why was it always necessary to compare everything with the Academy? No matter what happened he invariably seemed to be thinking back to Academy days, not always with regret, either.

Trying to stop it did no good. He must try harder, must end this business somehow.

Then Mr. Robinson placed his own paper before him. Turning it over he saw the mark on the back—B plus. Stacey, across the aisle, leaned across, took it from his desk, looked at the mark, and without saying a word but with an air of disgust which was plainly genuine, dropped it again. In some queer way Ronald felt ashamed of his paper. The teacher came toward them and slapped Stacey's down. Ronald couldn't help reading the large handwriting on the outside:

"This was stolen from the Encyclopedia."

There it was. He was shocked. Cheating, outright cheating, shocked him. He gasped. Stacey half-turned in his seat, looked over, glaring.

"Hey, what's the idea, you looking at my paper, huh?"

Ronny was confused, feeling Stacey's hostility and not for the first time. Painfully he realized the distance that separated him from that chattering roomful of boys and girls. To them he was a stranger; suspected by most, disliked by many. Look, he wanted to say, look, I don't like the boys at the Academy; they were my friends, they aren't anymore. I came down here to be one of you, to be friends with you, because I wanted to, of my own free will. But you . . .

They were laughing, paying no attention. He was still an outsider, that kid from the Academy, the football star who had beaten them last fall.

It was the football crowd he should have known, with whom ordinarily he would have been pals. Yet it was the football crowd who had never forgotten Meyer Goldman's injury. In the front row sat Dave Mancini, one of the tackles, who had merely nodded once and paid no more attention. At the side was Mike Fronzak, the right tackle, who never seemed to see him. At his left was Ned LeRoy who hardly noticed his presence in the room.

LeRoy wore a badly fitting, greenish sweater with a checked shirt underneath. His short curly hair receded from his high forehead; his square black jaw stuck out prominently. For several days Ronald had wanted to talk to him, but LeRoy never gave him any chance. If they passed in the corridors, LeRoy was always looking the other way. Never since his earliest days at the Academy had Ronald felt so lonely. They didn't give you the silent treatment here. They just never bothered about you. It was all impersonal. This place could be tough, too.

While the distribution of papers continued, there was a constant buzz and hum of conversation, a noise which would have meant a wholesale handing out of detentions at the Academy. However, no one seemed to mind and the teacher paid no attention. Once only did Mr. Robinson intervene.

"Aw, shut up," remarked Stacey in low-toned conversation with a boy behind.

Mr. Robinson, standing nearby, heard the remark. "Be polite, Jim. Say, 'Shut up, please!' " Stacey did not seem in the least bothered by this rebuke and continued his conversation.

Finally the papers were all distributed and the teacher made some comments on their English. The spelling, he announced, was bad. One thing the High School had in common with the Academy was bad spelling. Apparently every American boy and girl was a bad speller, and there wasn't much you could do about it. The teacher read some of their worst blunders, making Ronald smile.

"Now here's one word almost everybody slipped up on." He read from a student's paper in his hand. " 'The North denied the South the right to succeed.' " He chuckled. Ronald decided he liked this man. "I shouldn't blame the Southerners for being annoyed at this. What did he mean, class? Yes, that's it. Secede. How do you spell it?" Before Ronald thought, his hand was raised. Stacey turned with a sneer and he tried hastily to yank it down; but the teacher saw him. "Yes . . . Ronald . . . that's right. S-e-c-e-d-e. Some of you had queer ideas about that word and it's important. Here's another strange sentence. 'The farmers of this section were planting their opinions.' " The class roared.

He went on listing their mistakes, mistakes that Ronald found hard to understand. Simple things, such as the lack of margins at the top and sides of their papers. Sentences not punctuated. Most of these errors seemed elementary to Ronald. He lost interest and began looking around the room, at the huge class of girls and boys, at the words and problems written on the blackboard, at the notices stuck up on a smaller board in the rear of the room, at the Honor Roll of the class posted high above their heads. It contained four names.

> "Marion Sackett
> Rose Lake
> Jeanette Calahan
> Esther Neuman."

Girls, all girls. That was the way it was in every room all over the school. The girls seemed to take all the honors everywhere. Why were girls like that? And why did they invariably giggle, why couldn't they walk and talk together two minutes without giggling? In study periods—in the library—in the corridors—on the stairs between classes—in the cafeteria—giggle—giggle—giggle.

Yet not all were gigglers, either. There were several, quite noticeable in the room, who never giggled, who were sort of serious. Especially a tallish girl in the front of the room, a girl with blonde hair and red lips. In his first week at Abraham Lincoln Ronald had discovered that all the girls except the homely ones, who apparently didn't care, put on makeup. This girl usually wore the same costume; a rose-colored sweater and skirt, effective with her hair. She also wore stockings and tan and white shoes. He glanced under the desks around the room, looking over the bare legs, fat legs, short legs, scrawny legs, ugly legs, lovely legs. Ronald suddenly decided he was in favor of stockings.

Yes, he was in favor of stockings. He looked again at her legs; they were long and slender. His eyes went up to the rose-colored sweater which plainly defined her pretty figure. Just at that moment she turned, caught him staring, and smiled. Yes, smiled distinctly. He glanced behind. No, it was plainly for him, that smile. Because at the desks in the rear heads were bent down over books or else turned toward the windows. His face grew quickly warm. He buried his own head in a book so no one would notice his feeling.

The bell rang. A boy was reciting but he was not even permitted to finish his sentence. This was hard for Ronald to understand. No matter whether a teacher or a student was speaking, the bell was always the signal for a turmoil of chair-scraping, book-thumping, and general clatter to begin immediately. Nobody ever waited for the speaker to finish. Some things about Abraham Lincoln High he knew he would eventually accept and find normal. This, never.

He lowered his head once more over a pile of books, his face crimson still. The boys and girls swept past and he hoped they wouldn't look at him. He envied these boys their ability to talk to girls, to walk with girls, to stand around with girls naturally, never getting hot or red or embarrassed. At the Academy everyone got upset if they suddenly met a girl on Quad; everyone that is except the wolves. The wolves were on the lookout for girls all the time; they'd go downtown for a coke in the afternoon just to date the girls. Athletes weren't wolves. If you played football you had no time for wolfing.

There was a faint smell of scent; pleasant, soft. She was standing beside him. Nice eyes, blue, large. Quite tall, and he liked tall girls. He rose. As he did, the pile of books on his desk slipped off and fell to the floor. She laughed and he had to laugh also.

"I'm Sandra Fuller. You don't remember me, do you?"

From the door Stacey was looking back, shouting something over his shoulder, something that fortunately was lost in the noise. He mumbled a few words because he really didn't remember; except vaguely that her face was a face he had seen before.

"I met you at the Junior Prom at the Academy last fall. Remember, I was with Eric Rodman."

Remember! Why, of course he remembered; he remembered all right; he remembered a vision of white, a girl who had seemed even taller than this but no more attractive; he remembered a wonderful dancer, and most of all he remembered Eric's sour grin as he kept cutting in.

"Sure, sure I remember. I mean I didn't recognize you, but I remember you now all right."

They were moving out the door together, down the corridor, laughing. Really High School wasn't so bad after all. It was grand to find a friend, especially this friend, someone beside Gordon Brewster. The black-haired boy had attached himself to Ronny and tagged around with him ever since his first days. Ronald felt happy at having someone beside Gordon as a friend.

Her voice dropped but nevertheless he heard her distinctly. ". . . in that game . . . you were wonderful . . . I never thought . . . you'd win . . . definitely I never did. . . ."

He looked up quickly. She meant it. Yes, she certainly meant it. Did she know his part in the Goldman accident? No evidence of it, nothing in her look which said so. Then from the rear came that same voice, high-pitched, penetrating.

"Oh . . . Pretty Boy . . . oh, Ronny . . ."

He turned sharply. Usually he paid no attention; this time he was angry. Let me catch that guy and I'll kill him. Let me get my hands on him and I'll beat him up. I surely will. Standing on his toes and looking over the heads of the boys and girls in the rear, he attempted to glance back. Several of them around were laughing, for everyone had heard it, but there was no way of identifying the speaker or guessing whether he was the same one as before.

Later that day he was upstairs after school in the long corridor on the third floor shutting his locker. Gordon Brewster, whose locker was nearby, came over.

"Say! Know who's riding you? I do."

"No! Do you really! Who is it . . . Wait a minute. Hold on now." Maybe after all it was best not to know. To forget the whole thing. Often at the Academy he had seen this technique practiced, and there was only one way to beat it. Just pretend you never heard and keep on pretending. Give those birds the least satisfaction and they'd never let up. "Nope. No thanks, Gordon. I really don't care to know." He slammed his locker shut and started away down the corridor.

For several days Gordon had either been near his locker or waiting after school at the head of the stairs as he came down to go home.

"Ok, jess as you say, Ronald." He panted

along beside Ronny who was taking big steps, anxious to get out and away. Down the stairs, along the corridor to the main door. Outside the exit stood Stacey in the sunshine. He looked at them scornfully as they left the building together.

"Hey! I'm gonna ride along with you as far as West Avenue. Do you mind?" asked Gordon.

"Who? Me? No."

He did mind, though. Why did he mind, he wondered, as he got his bike from the rack; why did he care? For one thing he was tired of the kid who for more than a week had been sticking to him in the cafeteria, after school, between classes. Ronald was not at all certain he enjoyed having Gordon as his only friend at Abraham Lincoln High. No, that wasn't true. Not his only friend now. Sandra. Sandra Fuller. What a wonderful name. It fitted her, too. So she had seen him at the game in the fall. Then she must have seen the runback of that kick, and the touchdown.

They rode down Harrison Street together. "I'll only go as far as West Avenue. I'll see you tomorrow, Ronald, can I?"

"Tomorrow?" He was puzzled and also somewhat annoyed. Was this going to be a steady thing? "Why sure. Only what's the matter? Something wrong at school, Gordon?"

For a few yards they pedaled along in silence. Then the black-haired boy replied. "It's Stacey, see. He says he's gonna beat me up."

"Stacey! What's he got against you? What did you ever do to him?"

"Nothing. He's that way, that's all. Says he doesn't like me. Says if he catches me he'll sure beat me up. He will, too. He tried it on Goldman last year but Goldman was too big for him. But he did it to one kid. Here's West. I'm all set here. G'bye, Ronald. See you tomorrow."

He rode off alone down the sloping street, fast, faster, and disappeared around a corner.

4

His dad looked over at him, took off his glasses and put down the evening newspaper. A bad sign.

"You mean to say they cheat?"

The words sounded cruel and wrong. Ronald found an answer difficult.

"Why, no, not exactly that, Dad. See, at the Academy classes were smaller and the teachers could see everything. Here they can't."

"But wasn't there an honor system, or some such thing in effect there? How'd that work out?"

"It worked out ok, I guess. In exams they just trusted you. If a guy cheated, we gave him the silent treatment, that's all. At Abraham Lincoln the teachers patrol the class during tests, and it's sort of fun to fool 'em."

"Fun!"

"Aw, Dad, you know, you remember. You used to fool your teachers. It's a kind of game. Everybody does it. Besides, they snoop around. So the kids all do."

"Yes, but you aren't fooling the teacher. You're fooling yourselves."

Ronald was far from impressed. He had heard this before. "That's what they keep on saying. They always say that. But just the same . . ."

"Look here, Ronald." His father lit a cigarette. Ronald wished he had gone to his room and turned on the Fred Allen program. This was going to be unpleasant. "Tell me about your work. How about your schoolwork? How's it coming along?"

"He's brought his books home tonight for the first time in a week!" His mother, always at the wrong moment. "He never brings his books home anymore."

"Is that right? How's it happen you don't study at home, Ronald? You had to work every night at the Academy; it's a fine thing to get habits like that. I'm afraid you're neglecting your studies."

"Oh, no, Dad. I'm not, not at all. You're wrong."

"But you've been out three or four nights a week lately. I've noticed it, your mother has noticed it."

"Oh, no, Dad. I think you're mistaken. I'm not neglecting my work at all. Why I got an A on that last English paper, a B plus in the history test, and an A . . ."

"Well, Ronald." His mother became determined. "You don't mean to say you work the way you worked at the Academy."

"Mother! You don't understand. I don't hafta."

"Have to, Ronald, not hafta. I do hope you won't use the slovenly English those boys at High School . . ."

"Oh, Mother . . ."

His father, however, was far more interested in the problem of his work than his grammar. "Look here, how do you mean you don't have to work, Ronald?"

" 'Cause I don't, that's all. 'Cause I know the stuff, most of it. If not, I can always do it in my first study period at school."

"Then you mean it's easier?"

"I dunno, I guess so. Yes, the work's easier. At Abraham Lincoln they give you a chapter of history instead of three chapters, or thirty lines of Latin instead of eighty-five like we got everyday at the Academy. See! I can get it all, the lessons I mean, in my study periods."

Again his mother had to say something. "But that rainy afternoon last week when I called for you in the car I noticed all the girls took piles of books home with them."

"The girls! The girls! Of course the girls take books home. What else have they got to do 'cept paint their fingernails? We fellows have to do sports and things. You didn't notice any boys taking books home, I bet."

"But, Ronald . . ." His father was interested now. Funny, the sort of things which interested older people. Imagine anyone being interested in lessons. Yet his father was interested in the Tigers, too. "But, Ronald, suppose you weren't prepared."

"I am prepared. Anyhow it's different at Abraham Lincoln."

"How is it different?"

"Well, at the Academy if you aren't prepared you get a detention. That means you just don't go out for baseball practice. You stay in with the teacher all afternoon and work. If you misspell a word you have to write it down fifty times after school. Here, if you misspell a word, they just tell you it's wrong, and the kids say, they say, 'Aw, I can spell it right.' "

"Don't they give you detentions at Abraham Lincoln?"

"No. 'Nother thing, the classes are so big you don't get called on so often."

"I see. You don't have to be prepared."

"But I am prepared, Dad. I know the stuff ok. Point is, most of the fellows don't half the time; they aren't so well prepared as we were at the Academy."

"Where you had no girls and no movies and nothing to do except get your lessons for the next day."

"Gee, Mother . . ."

"How many in your classes, did you say, Ronald?"

"Well, Dad, that depends. In French and algebra they're smaller. In the others they're pretty large. Now in English, for instance, there's about thirty-five or more. See, the teacher has so many kids she doesn't get around to everyone in her class. Miss Davis, in English, for instance. They say she has about three hundred themes to read and correct before Christmas, so she reads them all and grades them carefully the first time, and then gives you about the same mark the rest of the year."

"Ronald! I don't believe it."

"The kids all say so, Mother; that's what the kids say."

The telephone rang. Ronny started quickly but his mother was quicker.

"Yes? Yes, just a minute." She half-sighed into the telephone. It was her girl-voice. He could always tell by that tone, a tone implying anything but cordiality. It was a wonder anyone ever called him. Were other boys' mothers like that? Probably not.

"Hullo."

" 'Lo, Ronny." There was a silence. Then he felt her presence, smelled again the pleasant odor of her clothes and her lipstick. "This is Sandra."

As if he needed to be told!

"Oh. G'd evening."

In the background his mother was making furious signs, pointing at the schoolbooks on the table in the hall where he'd dropped them. Her eyebrows were raised and she kept indicating the books. He understood her sign language well enough. Gosh, sometimes mothers were simply terrible.

"Uhuh . . . uhuh . . ."

Sandra continued, talking fast. Between his mother's movements and the surprise of the telephone call, he could hardly understand what the girl was saying. Could he what? Could he come over for a little while? Inside something went thump-thump-thump. He found it hard to reply. His mouth was dry. It made no difference, for she continued without pause.

". . . Have you heard Artie Shaw's . . . Concerto for Clarinet . . . you heard it . . . you haven't?"

"Yes . . . I mean . . . well, I guess not."

"An' I got Cab Calloway's 'Jumping Jive.' Don't you just love him, Ronny? An' his 'Minnie the Moocher.' Oh, definitely, I love him . . ."

"Yeah, he's snazzy."

"Do you know the house?" Know the house! Of course he knew the house. He knew the house all right. "It's the one with honeysuckle in front of the porch." Again something went funny inside Ronny. That honeysuckle vine was noticeable from the street. It had a long swing hammock behind it, well concealed from the street. And the other way round, thought Ronny.

"Yeah. Uhuh. Uhuh." That seemed to be about all he could manage to get out. How could you talk to a girl when your mother was doing a one-act show with eyes and hands right in front of you?

"Then you'll be right over?" There was almost anxiety in her voice, and he felt queer for the third time.

"Ok. G'bye." The telephone was hardly down when his mother spoke.

"Now, Ronald." Whenever she began in that tone it meant trouble. Oh, gosh. "Now, Ronald. You must *not* go out this evening. Please forbid him to go out, Dad."

That's it. Passing the buck to Dad. Gee, this was terrible. This was worse than the Academy. A fellow had a call from his girl, and his parents acted like . . . like it was a reform school.

Unexpectedly his father came to his rescue. "No, I won't forbid Ronald to go out. He knows better than either of us whether or not he can afford to go out. You've got to let him assume responsibility for his own acts. . . ."

"But he's been out twice this week already,

once to that stamp club and then to the movies. Now these girls!"

"It's not either these girls, it's Sandra Fuller."

"Sandra Fuller?"

"Yes."

"Well, whoever she is, she can't be a nice girl, pestering you at home like this. If I'd called your father up . . ."

"Oh, Mother . . ."

"Now, now. Look here, this is entirely up to Ronald. He should make his own decisions. He knows he can't even take his College Boards for Yale unless he gets A's and B's in all his studies. He must stand at the top of his class."

"But, Dad, I told you, I got a B in the last history test; B plus it was, honest I did."

"All right, all right. It's up to you, Ronald. You're old enough to be on your own now. You chose to leave the Academy and go to High School. So you must decide these things for yourself. If you feel able to go out tonight, that's your responsibility."

It was a responsibility he felt quite willing to accept. Why not? The French was a pipe; he knew that. The history was easy, too. The English theme could be done without trouble in his first study period. Of course the Latin was harder. Yes, that was harder. And Mrs. Taylor was plenty strict. True, the lessons were shorter than those at the Academy; but the one for tomorrow was really difficult, and she expected you to know it. It began *Quid nunc Catilina.* Not to be laughed off.

Oh, well. The thought of Sandra's hair, blonde, down the back of her neck, and that rose-colored sweater, and the hammock behind the honeysuckle on the porch pushed the next day with its Latin class from his mind. He went upstairs.

Thank goodness! There was one clean shirt in his drawer, his best one, too. Then a necktie. His were a sorry, messy lot, creased and wrinkled. He tiptoed into his father's room and took a brand-new tie, blue with gray stripes, a necktie that cost money. It matched his shirt perfectly and his best blue suit. Downstairs his mother was still talking, and he could hear words and sentences rising from the living room.

". . . These girls today . . . never get into college, he'll never . . ."

He wet his hair, brushed it, put on his suit coat, and in order to avoid more conversation and more complication did not go down the front way but sneaked out by the back stairs. This meant he could not go into the hall closet for his coat; but fortunately the evening was warm. Out the back door for his bike. Ordinarily with Dad in that mood he could have asked for the car and probably got it. However, what with the necktie and his mother's unconstructive attitude, he decided it best to say nothing and remain unseen.

It was a longish ride, even longer than he realized, and uphill much of the way. Already a drizzle had set in which made the going slippery and slow. His suit most probably'd be all out of press when he got there, too. At last he saw the corner ahead. There was the house, right beside the street light. He noticed as he put the bike inside the yard that the honeysuckle shielded the hammock from the light.

He was hot, and paused a minute to wipe off his face. Darn it, no handkerchief. You always forgot things when you were hurried. Shaking the mud from his spattered trousers, he went up the porch and fumbled for the bell. Inside there was a tinkle. Soon the door would open and she'd be there to greet him. He straightened the knot of his necktie.

Actually it was a long while before anyone appeared or there was any movement within. Suddenly the porch around him lit up and the door opened. It was not Sandra.

"Good evening."

" 'Evening. I'm Ronald Perry."

She stood smiling pleasantly. "Oh, yes, I think I've heard Sandra speak of you."

This was better. But still she didn't ask him inside. There was an unpleasant silence.

"Did you want to see Sandra?"

Did he want to see her! What a question! "Yes'm."

"I'm afraid she isn't at home this evening. She went out riding with a boy and two girls who called for her. Did she expect you?"

Once more he was warm all over. Only this was a different kind of warmness. It was the kind of warmness he had felt alone and exposed in the cafeteria when his tray had fallen to the floor. The warmness of confusion and disgust. It was also the warmness of disappointment. Perspiration trickled down his forehead.

"Yes'm. I mean, no'm." What was he saying? He stumbled backward down the steps, embarrassed and awkward, hardly hearing her words.

". . . So sorry, she'll be so sorry to have missed you. She's spoken of you . . . I remember . . ."

"Yes'm. Yes'm . . . good-bye . . . er . . . goodnight, yes'm."

He picked up his bike, tripped over the spokes, and tore his best blue trousers. Heck! Now look! Well, there you are. Women are like that. He went to the curb, yanked at his bike and sat down on the seat, ready to push off. It was disagreeably damp. By this time the rain was coming down harder, and he put up the collar of his suit coat.

A car came slowly past under the street light, the one that didn't shine on the hammock on the porch because of the honeysuckle vine. It was an ancient T-Model Ford, all painted white with wisecracks written over it. At the wheel sat a figure with a familiar face. As the car slid past he recognized the straight red hair and grinning mouth of Stacey. Derision was written all over that freckled face.

"Oh, Ronny, hi-ya, Ronny!"

Ronald sat motionless on the wheel. The rain came down faster, oozing inside the collar of his coat and soaking his best shirt and that new striped necktie. He started to shove off when he noticed an enormous sign painted across the full length of the car. It said:

DON'T LAUGH! YOUR DAUGHTER MAY BE INSIDE

He looked in at the two girls as the car went slowly past. One was Sandra Fuller.

II

Gosh! You'd think these kids were about ten years old. Now at the Academy . . .

There were snickers when he slapped his coat into his locker, titters when he came downstairs to the first study period, snickers in every class throughout the day. Always behind his back, always so he could hear them. The school that morning did little else but whisper and titter and snicker over the happening of the previous evening. Everyone knew about it; Stacey had taken good care of that. Stacey and that Sandra woman.

Although Ronald had the first period free, with the events of the night before on his mind he found himself unable to work. Try as he would to concentrate, he was continually interrupted by snickers or whispers. Nor was he the only pupil unprepared, he discovered. Right at the start of the Latin class, Mrs. Taylor called on that grinning, red-haired idiot.

"Will you please begin this morning, Jim. Page 273, no, 274, first paragraph. *Antiquis temporibus dei et dea ob injurias . . .*"

Stacey, who up to that moment had been the recipient of considerable admiration for his feat of the previous evening, was silent. No wonder. Mrs. Taylor often crossed up the class by not starting at the opening lines of the lesson in order to see whether you had really done the work or only the first part. Suddenly Stacey came back to the class, to Abraham Lincoln, to reality.

"H'm, yes'm, h'm . . . now . . . in ancient times the . . ."

"Where do you see 'now,' Jim?"

"No'm . . . in ancient times . . . the gods and goddesses . . . on account of . . . no, because of . . . I mean on account of . . ."

"On account of is quite correct."

"On account of . . ." There was a longish pause. "Oh, yes, on account of the . . . the . . . the . . ." He hesitated, scowling at the printed page before him.

"*Ob injurias supplicam,*" said Mrs. Taylor expectantly. But she was not a teacher to fool with. Some teachers let you get away with anything; not Mrs. Taylor. She knew her stuff and knew immediately whether you knew yours. If you didn't, you were in for trouble. Ronny buried his head in his book, wishing for the hundredth time since the previous evening that he had taken the advice of his mother and stayed home to work.

Mrs. Taylor broke into Stacey's mumblings. "Well, Jim, it's quite apparent you were not studying last night." She looked up quickly from her desk as a titter ran over the entire classroom.

"Ruth? Tommy? No? Unprepared? What's the matter with this class today? Ronald Perry, will you help us out, please. Translate, starting at the top of page 273."

Ordinarily it would have been simple. Often at the Academy he had done longer and harder assignments on sight; but with that girl watching from her seat up front, with Stacey slumped in his chair across the aisle, scowling and muttering phrases that drew subdued snickers, Ronny felt rattled. His voice was dry and hollow, his tone uncertain.

Mrs. Taylor interrupted. She stood no fooling.

You knew your stuff—or you didn't. This time her remark cut him. "Evidently you were out last evening also, Ronald."

Now the class roared. It was no subdued titter, it was not a ripple of amusement shared among themselves, it was a hearty laugh that swept the entire room. If anyone did not know about the evening's episode, it was, Ronald saw again, no fault of Stacey's. Only Mrs. Taylor failed to get the point. She looked up in astonishment now, glancing around the class and wondering what she had said to cause such merriment.

The laughter continued. Everyone laughed except Ronald. Mrs. Taylor made a mark in her classroom book. He knew what this meant. She was giving him an X for being unprepared, almost the first X he had received since coming to Abraham Lincoln High.

The moment the class ended, Sandra came toward him; but he grabbed his books and fled. She was the one person he wished to avoid.

The snickers and titters followed him all day, even upstairs while he tried miserably to eat in the cafeteria where Gordon Brewster insisted on sitting at his side. From the adjoining tables he could hear remarks and whispers, and finishing his meal in silence he refused to talk to Gordon. Silently also he went down to Mr. Horvath's class in algebra, Gordon panting along at his heels like a trained dog.

Latin was one thing, algebra was another. For just a few minutes the titters disturbed him when Mr. Horvath asked him to come to the board and solve a problem. The back of his neck felt red and his face was hot; but this disappeared as soon as he got into the working of the equation. Before long he forgot about the class behind, solved it, and putting down the chalk returned to his seat.

"Yes . . . that's right; now, Stacey . . . will you please try the next one. On page 49." Unlike the other teachers, Mr. Horvath always called you by your last name.

Jim stumbled up, his red hair bristling, his face determined. He wiped off Ronald's slanting handwriting in such a way as to arouse a chorus of snickers over the entire room. Then he put some figures on the board. Mr. Horvath, watching from the side where he was leaning against a windowsill, interrupted.

"X *over* 2? Is that correct? X *over* 2? Can't you even state the problem correctly, Stacey?"

The redhead wiped out the figures hastily with a sweep of his arm and substituted the right ones. Then he stepped back a little, looked at the blackboard, stood there for a minute, came closer and began writing. After a bit he hesitated and erased it all once more. At last he went to work.

"No, no, no, that's not it at all, Stacey." The voice of the teacher was exasperated. Ronny liked this man; he also knew his stuff and allowed no fooling. His discipline was strict, he permitted no talking, and was death on copying and cheating. "We have no time to waste today; this is a long lesson." He bent over his black classroom book. Aha, thought Ronny, giving him an X.

"It looks to me, Stacey, as if you weren't studying last night."

Like Mrs. Taylor he was wholly unprepared for the sudden outburst that followed. Jim, who had put the chalk down with relief and started for his seat, grinned at the noise. The teacher still leaning against the windowsill looked up at the quick roar of the class, that little black book in his hands. "I see nothing funny in this." The class did. They laughed again, and louder. All, that is, save Ronald.

Mr. Horvath shook his head, realizing that

something was going on which he couldn't appreciate. He made the telltale mark in his book. There goes the X, thought Ronald, and serves Stacey right, too. There's some justice in things, anyhow.

"Gordon Brewster, will you solve this one for us?" The black-haired boy came forward eagerly, almost a little too eagerly. It was easy enough for Ronny to see why Stacey disliked him. With quick, competent gestures he erased the meaningless mass of figures left by his predecessor, and began writing. The chalk made screechy noises on the board.

"Please don't make the chalk squeak," said Mr. Horvath from the window. Gordon, engrossed in the task before him, half turned, inquiringly. "I say please don't make the chalk squeak, Brewster. Hold it by the end."

"Oh, yessir, yessir." He went on, more quietly. His fingers flew across the board. The figures grew, multiplied rapidly. At last he finished and turned toward the teacher by the window. There was a moment's silence while the class watched.

"Yes, that's it." His head went down once more as he entered a mark in his black book, and Gordon started for his seat. He had to pass

Stacey and at that exact moment, just as he had done in the cafeteria, the Irish boy stuck his foot into the aisle. Not much, but enough so Gordon tripped and would have fallen had he not reached out and caught Ronald's desk. The teacher looked up in the confusion, guessing what had happened.

"That'll do, Stacey. You better pay close attention to these problems; they're important. Remember you can't do them if you aren't prepared, and if you ever get behind in this class you'll have great trouble catching up. And don't forget, the baseball season's coming." This reference to baseball meant that unless he did better Stacey would fail in algebra and perhaps be unable to play. Stacey took the remark in silence and the class continued.

Finally the bell rang, the last of the day. From the room above, from those across the hall, from each side came the scraping of chairs, the banging together of books, the laughter and talk, that torrent of noise which meant liberation. Release from school and work and teachers and lessons for at least a few hours. Instantly the hall outside was filled with chattering groups.

Ronald hastily slapped his books in a pile and

dashed for the door. This time Sandra was right behind him.

"Ronald! Wait a minute. Please wait a minute."

He had no wish to wait, for her or anyone else. To get away, to get out and home as soon as possible was all he wanted, so he slipped into the hall before she could say another word. She was there, at his side, then in a few steps she was lost in that mob moving in both directions up and down the long corridor.

On the third floor he stopped for a minute at the water fountain, and while leaning over heard Stacey's voice booming nearer. As he straightened up the red hair went past. Ronald walked down the hall behind him. As usual Stacey was amusing himself at the expense of Gordon Brewster.

"Hey! Quit that, will ya, Stacey?" Gordon, just ahead, turned to remonstrate but was laughed off.

"Aw, go on, you cluck—you."

Stacey continued walking close behind Gordon, stepping on his heels every few feet. Ronald reached his locker and paused. He leaned over. 8. 17. 9. He opened it, threw in his notebook and algebra, took out the Cicero, the French grammar, and reached inside for his coat.

"Hey, Ronny. Wait a sec." Gordon was panting at his side.

"Yeah."

"I'm gonna go home with you, ok?"

No! Not ok. Not ok at all. Ronny wanted to be alone, to stay by himself more than ever, yet there was an appeal in that voice he could not resist. The note of fear in it angered him, too, and as he straightened up from his locker he noticed the frightened look on the face of the other boy. This kind of thing must stop. Meyer Goldman was right; there's only one thing, stand up to the guy. Don't let him get away with it.

"Ok."

Gordon's face brightened. He shifted the pile of books he was carrying from one arm to the other. He always took more books home than any six boys in school.

At this moment Stacey went past. Seeing them in conversation, his glance fell contemptuously on the books under Gordon's arm. Making a quick step toward them, he reached out and with a swift jab sent the whole pile toppling to the floor. The books rolled beneath the feet of the passing crowd.

This was enough. He was tired of it all. Tired of the eternal "Oh, Ronny . . ." up and down the corridors, tired of having Gordon Brewster tag along whenever he went into the library, the cafeteria, or the boys' room. And he was tired of Stacey. Most of all he was tired of Stacey and his annoying tricks. So he moved in. The freckled face came closer.

"What's the idea, Stacey?"

"Idea of what?"

Several boys going past stopped. There was a sudden quietness over the noisy corridor as if the crowd felt the approach of trouble. All around, the movement of boys and girls, the calling and shouting and whang-banging of lockers, died away.

"Idea of rushing this kid all the time."

"Yeah . . . an' who's to stop me?"

"Me. Right now. Cut it out, see?"

The group, now larger, moved in closer. Gordon somewhere behind tugged anxiously at his sleeve.

Stacey's face became red. "You! You stop me? I'd like to see you try it, you big jerk."

Relief. He had to have relief. Relief could only come in action, quick, expressive. He forgot the boys and girls and other boys on the outside peering over shoulders, forgot where he was and what he was doing in the satisfaction of his fist on Stacey's jaw. The red face reeled back, then came in, the eyes clouded with moisture, yet cold and savage. All at once he felt the pain of Stacey's knuckles on his nose, a sharp, violent pain. He staggered.

Then the lights went out. There was no more pain.

III

"Just don't move. Stay perfectly still, don't move." The voice was up there, way up there, up, up, above, up there.

Who said anything about moving? He didn't have the slightest desire to move. Wanted to stay like that, there, motionless, forever. And ever. Up there were more voices, older voices, vaguely familiar voices floating through a film. Let's see, where is this? The Academy? Nope, not the Academy. It's home. Yes. No, not home either. It's Abraham Lincoln. That's stone, it's cold, it's the floor, the tiled stone floor. That's it, Abraham Lincoln. Abraham Lincoln, Washington, Jefferson . . .

This was like waking from a dream. Someone, several hands on each side, grasped him. He was thrown through the air, thrown, that's what it felt like. Pains shot through his head, violent pains. Hey, lemme alone, you fellas. Lemme be. Just let me stay there, motionless on the stone floor. Why didn't they let him stay where he was, forever and ever? And ever.

Instead he was pulled, hauled, jostled, thrown. All the while those terrible pains in his head, so bad he didn't want to talk. He wanted only to be let alone. Please let me alone, that's all. A man in a white coat leaned over and asked him something but he didn't want to talk. Go away. Let me alone, please; just let me alone, that's all.

Now where was he? He woke up, looked around. It was a room. It wasn't the floor, the stone floor, the cold floor; it was a room, a strange room, and he was in a bed. Not certainly his own room in the Academy. No, nor his room at home either. Sunshine was sweeping into this room and a woman in white had his wrist. A nurse. Doggone, this is the hospital. Yep, sure as sure, it's the hospital. She leaned over.

"Just don't try to talk."

Now why did everyone say that? He had no desire to talk, the fact was that he never felt less like talking. The pains were still there, but not so close, far away, sort of. He felt them only as in a dream, not pounding and terrible inside his head. He was in a dream. A dream, that's it. He was going back to sleep.

When he woke it was all different; night, and his mother was there, and then Dad. More sleep, and finally the light once more. Drip, drip, the rain spattered against the window. He felt better. The pain had almost gone. So had that strange faraway feeling, as if he was here and his body over there, someplace far away. There was a nurse there, not the same nurse; another nurse in white, who kept doing useless things such as giving him orange juice and medicine to drink. Then doctors entered.

At last the whole thing came back clearly; the fight, the ring of boys standing around, the pain of Stacey's fist just before the lights went out. He looked about the room curiously. It was full of flowers and the nurse was arranging them. From the class. From the principal. These were, she read the tag, from Gordon Brewster.

That afternoon he saw his mother who didn't

say much. As he was tired he said little, too. The next day, however, he really felt better, able to eat and sit up a little. His mother came and was cheerful.

"It's wonderful; the X-rays don't show a thing, Ronald."

"X-rays! When did they take those?"

"That first afternoon you were brought in. You didn't know much what was going on then. The doctors were all afraid of a fracture of the skull; but there wasn't any, thank heavens."

Fracture of the skull. It sounded bad. Something that was always happening to someone else, in football or hockey. The nurse entered. "There's a Mister Stazy or Stacy, or something, says he wants to see you as soon as he can."

His mother went out to meet him, and a minute later Stacey came in alone. His red hair was stiffer and straighter than ever, but over his usually grinning freckled face was a solemn and worried look. He didn't seem the same Stacey.

"Gee, Ronald . . ." His face sobered even more at the sight of the bed.

"Hi there, Stacey . . ." Funny, the mere exertion of talking tired him. Just talking was hard work. Stacey stood there, awkwardly, saying nothing, staring at him with open eyes. Now he, Ronald, was on the receiving end. Or was it Stacey? That was it, Stacey was on the receiving end. You had to go through things of this sort really to understand.

The redhead came closer to the bed. "Gee, Ronald, I feel bad about this. You dunno how bad I feel . . ."

Same thing, only with Stacey on the receiving end this time. Same thing, same words. Wasn't that about all he could stammer out one morning last fall in front of Meyer Goldman and his father? Gee, Goldman . . . yes, he knew how Stacey felt.

"Forget it, Jim. It's ok. I hit you first, anyway; I had it coming to me." First, last, what difference did it make? When you knocked a man out, it was all the same. He knew, he understood how that stammering Irish boy felt. Why, only a few months ago he had felt exactly the same in the same kind of a room on the same floor of this same building. Didn't some teacher somewhere say that history repeated itself?

"Aw, say, Ronald, look here . . . look, you're coming ok, aren't you? You're gonna come through all right. . . ."

"Sure. Sure I'm ok. It just knocked me out, that's all. Seems like those tiled floors are harder than my head." He tried to laugh, he did laugh, and a twinge of pain shot up the back of his neck. He moved uneasily. Stacey noticed it immediately.

"No fooling! Honest to goodness, are you better? Are you? Look, Ronald, I didn't mean to lay you out on purpose, honest I didn't. I just got mad and hit back, that's all."

Same words, same situation, same feeling. He knew, he understood. You had to go through things like this, to hit a man and almost cripple him, you had to be on the receiving end before you understood.

"I getcha, Jim. Don't worry; it's nothing, and I'm all right." Then a thought struck him. "Hey, Jim! Sorta looks like we're all square now, doesn't it?"

Stacey was puzzled at first. Then he got it. "Oh. You mean for Meyer Goldman?"

"That's it."

"Uhuh. Guess so. Say, you understand, don't you, Ronald? You understand how it was?"

"I understand, better'n you could think, Jim. Just forget it all."

"An' about Brewster. Gee, I'm sorry I pestered that kid. I never realized, exactly. Only sometimes he just sort of, well, I dunno, he sort of . . ."

"Yeah. I understand. He's irritating often, that kid is. He doesn't mean to be."

"I know. I've cut that all out; it's over, see, Ronald?"

"That's fine, Jim. I'm glad."

"So hurry up and get well, will you? We're gonna have some ball team this spring; we could sure use you out there in the field. Practice begins next week, so try and make it."

It was the first time anyone at Abraham Lincoln had needed him or said they needed him. Also the first time anyone had spoken of the school as "we" to him. He wanted to say something, but just then the nurse poked her face in the room and began making signs to Stacey. Then he noticed there were pains in his head once more.

"Yeah, an' one more thing." Stacey edged toward the door. "She never called you up at all, Ronny; she never did it."

Ronny sat up. The sudden movement sent a burst of pain up the back of his head; but he didn't care. "What d'you mean? She didn't . . ."

Somehow he couldn't bring himself to mention her name. "She didn't? What d'you mean; how d'you mean, Jim?"

"Nope. She never knew a thing about the whole affair. It was all my gag. All of it. I planned it, see, 'cause I saw she liked you from the first day you came to Abraham Lincoln. So I got Helen Kempner, that's the big girl with glasses, the one she's always going round with; you know the one, don't you?"

Ronald knew. From his earliest days at the Academy he had noticed that good-looking girls always went around with homely ones. That's how girls were.

"Yeah. Uhuh, I remember her."

"Well, she's the one who called you up that night, 'cause she can talk like Sandra, see. Then she went and got Sandra to come riding with us, and I showed up there at the corner just when I knew you'd come along. She never knew a thing about it. Honest."

"Oh!" A weight fell off. Then he hadn't been framed. It wasn't at all what he had supposed.

"Say! That's good. I'm mighty glad you told me, Jim. Honest, I feel better about it."

"Yep. I thought I oughta tell you all this. 'Nother thing. Here's the latest number of the school paper, you'd be sure to see it sometime anyway. It was all made up and ready to print before . . . before the accident. So don't pay attention to what it says there about you, will you? Remember that evening was all my idea, every bit of it. Well, I gotta shove along. Get outa here quick, Ronny; we sure need you in that-there team."

"You bet, Jim. I'll be back soon, won't I, nurse?" The nurse didn't hear. She was urging Stacey toward the door.

He leaned back, his head aching now. Well, it was almost worth it, all of it, the pain, the discomfort, the absence from school with all that Latin for Mrs. Taylor to make up; why, that alone would mean lots of evenings working at home. Yet it was worth it to know what had really happened. To know she had never called him up, that she hadn't fixed it with Stacey, hadn't pulled a fast one. What did it matter if they laughed, if the school paper wrote it up? He looked at the copy of the *Mercury* left on the bed.

"Speaking as we were above of wolves, what

a wolf our new junior acquisition from the Academy, Ronald Perry, turned out to be! At present he is wolfing in the direction of Sandra Fuller. We hear she loves to date him. (But definitely.)"

5

He walked down the corridor with its gray and black square tiles on the floor and the murals of baseball, football, and basketball on the side walls. How fresh and new and clean it was; how strange and different all this had seemed that first morning back in January. Now it was familiar. Those figures hitting home runs and throwing passes had once seemed amazing; now he hardly noticed them in his daily movements about the building. Except when, as today, he'd been away from the place a while. He passed the drinking fountain set back at one side. On the second floor there was another fountain just like it, and above that on the third floor another, near his locker where the fight had occurred. The strangeness of the place was gone. He was coming back to a school he knew.

And to people he knew. They surged toward him down the hall, girls in sweaters with their arms intertwined, boys in windbreakers and checked shirts. They all spoke, some of them half-eagerly, and many stopped him. He was a stranger no more.

"Hullo, there, Ronny . . ."

"How you feel, Ronald?"

"Hey, Ronny, you ok again?"

"Can you play ball, Ronny? Will they leave you play ball now?"

"Will they let you play, will they?"

"Hullo, Ronald. Everything all right?"

"Hi there, Ronny, how you feel?"

"Hullo, Mac. Hullo, George, glad to see you. Yeah, I'm ok. How are you, Chester? . . . Hullo, Mike. . . . Hullo, Ruth. . . . Hullo, Dave. Sure I'm ok. Yep, I'm gonna play baseball if I'm good enough to make the team. Why, sure I mean it.

Hullo, Gene. Hullo, Susie. Hullo, Ned, why, Ned, how are you?"

The Negro shuffled up with his hand held out in a friendly gesture. Golly, he's actually smiling, thought Ronald. That's something, isn't it? Takes a man being knocked out to make that kid grin.

And look, there's Meyer! Meyer without that horrible leather neckpiece. "Why, Meyer, how are you, boy? Gee, it's good to see you again! How long you been back? You have? That's super. Me? Sure I'm ok; don't I look ok? Well, I am. Sure I'll play ball; I will if I'm good enough. . . ." It was great to have Meyer in school. Ronald had seen so much of him in a bedroom with that leather neckguard that he hardly looked natural without it.

Then from a distance he saw a familiar freckled face topped by a bristle of straight red hair approaching. Some of the crowd standing around saw him coming also and moved aside as he drew near.

"Hey! Hey there, Ronny!" He waved.

"Hullo, Jim." Then he felt himself grabbed by the arm.

"Here we are, all three of us together." Now he had Meyer by one arm, too.

"That's right, Ronny . . ."

"Yessir, that's right. Here we are, all three of us together." Arm in arm, that was the way they moved down the corridor. Stacey in the middle, Ronald on one side, and Goldman on the other.

"There's a musical assembly in the auditorium. The band'll play and the Glee Club'll sing. It's for the Scholarship Fund. You got ten cents, you guys? C'mon." They were moving toward the crowd at the door, a crowd that had for some time been pushing in.

"C'mon." He grabbed their arms again and together the three went down the aisle.

Someone called to Ronald. He heard his name, his first name. "Hey, Ronny, hey there, Ronny. . ." He felt Stacey's arm, tight in his own. It made him warm and comfortable inside, it almost gave him a kind of glow. At last he was one of them, he was a part of the school, he was a stranger no more. They moved into their seats, Stacey in the middle, Ronald on one side and Goldman on the other. That was the way they sat all the rest of their time at Abraham Lincoln High.

In between classes later on it was the same thing. Boys he hardly knew, girls he had hardly seen, came up to welcome him back, to say they were glad he was well and with them again. They greeted him on the narrow stairs, in the long corridors, in the library, in the cafeteria. At lunch Jim slouched over with his tray and sat down next to Ronny.

"Now look here, Ronald, what are we going to do about this-here kid, Brewster?"

"I know. I was thinking about that. I've been thinking about him a whole lot. He sticks closer than a Scotch uncle; in fact he got so on my nerves last month . . ."

"Same here. After you . . . after, I mean while you were in the hospital he changed over to me, and I had him all day—morning, noon, and night."

"You telling me! Well, I have an idea, or sort of an idea, about that kid. What do you say to this, Jim? It would take up some time and do him lots of good, too, if, now, we went to work and made him . . ."

"Hullo, Ronny. Hullo, Jim. Mind if I sit opposite you guys?"

"Why, hullo, Gordon. No, of course not. Sit down."

"Sure, sure, sit right down, Gordon. About that thing, Jim, I'll talk to you and tell you my ideas after the next period."

When school was over, Ronald walked upstairs to his locker. This time Gordon was not waiting; on the contrary, he had to go to Gordon's locker down the hall to find him. As usual that energetic student was piling up a Mount Everest of books to carry home.

"Hi there, Ronny! You don't have to wait. I don't need to ride home with you anymore; me and Jim are friends now."

"I know all that; but justa same, Gordon . . ."

"Jim's swell to me now; we get on all right. You don't need to wait, Ronny, honest you don't."

"Yes, I know that, Gordon. But Jim and I want to ride a ways home with you. If you don't mind, that is, Gordon."

"No. Of course not." At the bottom of the stairs Jim was waiting. They left the building, got their bikes, and started down Harrison. Into West Avenue. They were nearing Gordon's usual turn.

"Well, s'long, you fellas. I'll see you tomorrow."

"Hold on, wait a minute, Gordon; we'd like you to come along with us a piece."

"Where? Which way? What for?"

"To the Y," said Jim and Ronny together.

"To the Y!" Gordon nearly fell off his bike.

There was a trace of alarm in his voice. "To the Y! What for?" He looked at them with concern. "What do you want me to go to the Y for?"

"You'll see." They rode on in silence. Down West Avenue into South Main to the traffic light and then up North Main. The brick Y loomed ahead. They yanked their bikes into the basement entrance.

"This is where we want to go, down here," said Jim. "Come on, Gordon." They passed through a small office, down a passageway, and opening a door entered a gymnasium. A man in white trousers and a white undershirt was pounding a bag.

Rat-tat-tat, rat-tat-tat-tat-tat . . .

"Hey there, Jake." The man turned quickly, saw them, stopped, pulling off one glove.

"Hullo, kid." He shook hands with Jim.

"This is Ronny. Ronald Perry. He's a football halfback and a darn good one, and he packs a mean left, too. And this is Gordon Brewster, boy I spoke to you about over the phone."

"Say, what is this anyhow?" Gordon looked worried.

"Boxing. Boxing, see? Ronny and I, we figured what you needed was a little toughening up. So we arranged with Jake here . . ."

"But I don't want to box. I don't know how to box, I . . ."

"That's just it."

"And I don't want to know how. Besides, I've got to work. A history paper due tomorrow. And a book report for Thursday. I haven't cracked that book yet."

"Do you good, young fella," said the man called Jake, not in a reassuring tone.

"He'll take it. And like it. Now . . ."

"Tomorrow! Tomorrow!" cried the unhappy Gordon. "Not today, please, not today. I have too much work today, honest I have."

"Gordon, you've got to begin and you might just as well make up your mind to begin now. Three times a week you're to report down here at three in the afternoon to Jake, understand? It's only for half an hour, but we aren't afraid you'll be getting any detentions to keep you in, so be sure you come on the button."

"Another thing, Gordon." Stacey towered over him. "No sloping off, get me? If he doesn't show up regular, Jake, you just let one of us know. We'll get him if we have to leave a ball game in the middle of the eighth. Hey, Ronny?"

"That's correct. Take your coat off and roll up your sleeves, Gordon. And get to work. Good-bye, Jake. Be sure and treat him rough. So long, Gordon; don't hurt the Professor, whatever you do. Remember, three o'clock three times a week, Monday, Wednesday, and Friday. If he misses out one single day, we'll hear from you, Jake."

They were in the passageway again, through the little office, and at their bikes. Up and back on the street they walked along together, laughing.

"Bet he'll leave us alone now."

"I'll say. Boy, how he'll hate the two of us."

"Yeah. Well, it'll do him lots of good. Do us good, too."

"You said it. Do the school good. A swell idea of yours, Ronny."

"The idea was ok, but the thing was I didn't know any boxing instructor. How'd you get to know him so well he'd take on a kid like Gordon for nothing, Jim?"

"Me? Oh, well, it's like this. He knows me, Jake does. I took lessons from him four years running."

"You did! I never knew that."

"Sure. I got to know him pretty well. And I love boxing. You know I was lightweight champion of the Y last two years I was under him, and now he says maybe next year he'll enter me in the trials for the Golden Gloves. If I can only pick up ten pounds, he will."

"Good heavens! And you're the guy I pasted in the face. Out of that whole school, I had to pick on a fighter who's good enough to enter the Golden Gloves. Twelve hundred students, and I had to pick on you. . . ."

They laughed together. " 'At's all right, Ronny." He patted him on the shoulder as they paused by a traffic light at the corner of South Main. " 'At's all right, boy. You're the only person I can remember who got the first crack in on me, and I'm still tasting blood and teeth from that smack you handed out. So you did ok, boy, you did ok. Here's where I leave you. We'll keep after that kid, you and I, huh? Ok. S'long."

"You bet. So long, Jim. And thanks a whole lot." He walked his bike slowly down the street, smiling to himself. To think I had to pick on a Golden Gloves boxer! In all that school, with all those boys, to think I had to smack a guy who's the lightweight champion of the Y. No wonder he knocked me out. But to think I should have jumped down a guy's throat who turns out to be the best boxer in his class in town, and a Golden Gloves . . .

"Hey, Ronny . . ."

"Ronald!"

"Hey there, Ronald! Perry! Hey, Perry!"

He looked up. Familiar voices came through the traffic. Across the street they were waving. He saw them, waved back.

They came over, deftly dodging a line of cars and trucks. Keith in his checked jacket, Eric with a fawn-colored polo coat open at the neck, and Tommy Gilmore in a new blue suit. They all wore saddle shoes, and neckties striped blue and black. Those were the ties of Heptameron, the senior society. It meant they'd just been taken in at the spring elections. If he had stayed, he would now be wearing one of those striped blue and black neckties.

"Hi, fellas, how are you? Hullo, Eric, hi there, Keith, Tommy." It was the first time he had seen anyone from the Academy since the morning he had walked out of Keith's room forever. "What you people doing downtown here this time of day?"

"Baseball equipment."

"What?"

"Baseball equipment. We came down with the truck for the new uniforms and baseballs; they're at the express station and we need them today."

"Boy, will we have a team this year! That young Heywood is a real pitcher."

"You mean the kid that was right half last fall?"

"That's right. Say, he's a pitcher, Ronny."

"You bet he is; got a mean sinker."

"Yessir, we'll sure beat you guys this time, no mistake."

"Maybe," said Ronald. "Maybe. How's things on the Hill? How's the Duke and everyone?"

"Just fine."

"How are *you*, Ronald? We hear they beat you up pretty bad."

"Who beat me up?"

"Those lugs down at the High School. Your buddies down there."

"Well, they didn't. I mean I . . . that is . . . where did you hear that? Who told you that?"

"They ganged up on you and put you in the hospital, that's what we heard. Didn't they?"

"Yes, and fractured your skull?"

"No! Yes. I mean, does my skull look as if it had been fractured?" He was confused and disturbed. "Why, we had an argument, that's all. I fell and hit my head on the stone floor in the corridor."

"An argument! Get that one! He calls it an

argument. We were told a crowd ganged up on you because you came from the Academy and they thought you were a sissy."

"Well, they didn't, see? Here's what happened. Remember Jim Stacey, their end . . ."

"Oh, that goon."

"He's not a goon. He's a good guy, a real fella, and he's my friend, too. Also, he's the best boxer in town for his size, Keith. Well, we got into an argument—oh, all right, a fight if you like that word any better—and he knocked me out. That's absolutely all there was to it. . . ."

"If you make friends with lugs like that, you must expect brawls. . . ."

The traffic light was changing. What was the use? He planked his bike with force down beside the curb and jumped on. "I'm going uptown. So long, you fellas."

"So long, Ronny."

"Take it easy, Ronny."

"Hey, Ronald, tell 'em we got a real pitcher this year, with a sinker and everything."

He rode down South Main. Faster, faster. He was glad he wasn't wearing a blue and black Heptameron necktie.

II

Nine more outs. Only nine more outs and they would go against the Academy for the final game of the year, an undefeated team. Nine more outs, Mike, nine more outs, Chester, nine more outs, Jim. That's what everyone thought to himself when they dashed out for the end of the seventh. While the Bannister batter, tapping the dirt from his spikes, came to the plate.

"Nice and loose there, Jim."

"Cool and nervous, Jim-boy."

"Ok, Jim, let's us get this first man."

As Ronny trotted back toward his place near second, he could hear the coach yelling at them from the bench through cupped hands. Almost he sounded like a professional ballplayer.

"Lotsa pep out there, boys; lotsa pep alla time, Jim, alla time, Mike; talk her up, Bob. . . ."

"Ok, Jim, old boy, here's the easy man. This the one we want."

"Cool and nervous, Jim, alla time, Jim-old-boy-old-kid-old-boy . . ."

The tall Irishman in the box drew himself up and burned the ball into Mike Fronzak's mitt. The batter swung clean around, almost hitting the dirt, and drawing a barrage of noise from the entire field. Stacey watched as Mike leaned over, pulling up the tip of his chest protector to his stomach and giving the signals. Then he threw again. This time the batter caught it and hit a slow, dragging roller toward short, a hit that would have been safe on anyone but a fast shortstop with a sure arm. Ned LeRoy came in, perfectly balanced. With one movement he stopped the ball and without pause or hesitation shot it across to Bob Patterson on first. The umpire, still clutching his mask in his hand, ran down the path behind the batsman. Up shot his hand. A howl rose from the Bannister bench, but the man was clearly out.

In several minutes more they were trooping in toward the bench before the start of the eighth. Only six more outs now; six outs, Jim, six outs, Dave, six outs more, Bobby. They didn't say that because the coach wouldn't permit it; however, that's what everyone thought to himself. Only six more outs. While that one-run lead looked bigger than ever. Usually their scores ran into two figures. That day the pitchers were good and the fielding better, so the score was low.

Ronald squeezed in beside the coach on the

bench. "No, no, move down one, Ronny. I want LeRoy to sit next to me. And whatever you do, don't cross your legs."

Tom Quinn, the coach, was superstitious. He believed it was bad luck to talk about future games, to cross your legs while on the bench, and good luck to sit next to a Negro. When there was no Negro boy on the team, he always picked one in school to act as bat boy. This amused Ronny very much. At the Academy where there were separate coaches for every sport, baseball was coached by Mr. Spencer who taught ancient history. He had no superstitions, but instead a Harvard accent and a college background in baseball. No one ever got familiar with him.

At Abraham Lincoln one man coached baseball, football and basketball. Tom Quinn, a former all-American end at Indiana University, was tall, well built, and with his peaked cap down over his eyes looked exactly like a big leaguer. No wonder, for after leaving college he had played baseball with the Syracuse team of the International League. You wouldn't call the former center fielder of the Chiefs, Mr. Quinn. Naturally not. So you just called him Coach. That's what everybody called him.

Bud Talbot, the center fielder, popped up and then Ned drew a base on balls. Ronny leaned over for his bat.

"Watch me on every pitch, Ronald. And take the first one."

"Ok, Coach." His cap stuffed in his hip pocket, he stepped to the plate, hearing the cries from the field and the shout from the bench of the Bannister coach to his pitcher.

"Up and around his ears, Ike." Ronny was used to this one. Everyone threw high balls at him, figuring that because he wore no cap the glare of the sun would prevent his seeing them when they were high. It hadn't prevented his making the only extra-base hit of the game, nor kept him from standing third in the team batting average for the season.

The first pitch which he took was a ball. He turned, looking toward the coach on the bench. Hit it! Ok, I'll hit. He got a good hold and smacked a sizzling roller between first and second. The fielder made a stab for the ball, held it, and tossed quickly underhand to the shortstop on second who shot it in time to first. One out! Two out! The side retired.

Shoot! We wuz robbed. You wuz robbed,

Ronny, on that one. Hard luck, Ronny; hard luck, kid. Ok, gang, let's go now.

They ran out onto the field.

All right, Jim; c'mon now, Jim-boy, you can do it, Jim. Bear down now, Jim, old kid. This the man we want.

Jim bore down. He seemed to be getting better as the game went along. He struck the first batter out; the next man popped to Mike Fronzak.

Only four more outs, gang, only four to get. Here's their dangerous man, the captain and left fielder.

He hit the first ball between first and second, right in the slot. But Ronny, well back on the grass, knew he had a chance and started with the ball. Running with his head over, his gloved hand out as far as possible, he tried to reach the ball cutting through the thick spring grass. With a last effort he got to it, stabbed it, the ball resting in the webbing of his glove. But that rush carried him too far and fast. He tried to right himself, to stop; tottered, stumbled and almost fell. For a second he was sure he would fall. Staggering, he managed to recover enough balance to toss the ball over into Bob's waiting glove.

The runner thundered down the basepath, sore and angry at being cheated out of a hit. As he passed first, he came down hard on Bob's heel beside the bag. The big boy went down in a heap, and instantly the whole field became a pattern of motion. The coach, the umpire, the Bannister coach, the entire infield, ran across. Bob in pain on the ground was holding his foot in his hand.

"Naw . . . my ankle . . . my ankle . . . my ankle I tell you."

Someone shouted something at the Bannister runner who walked slowly down the foul line. "Aw, he oughta have kept his big hoofs outa the way." A fight seemed in the cards. But the Bannister coach stepped in. "Get back to the bench, Jake. You too, Sammy; all you boys. Get back there where you belong." Then he helped them carry Bob across and lay him on the grass behind their bench.

The coach leaned over and felt of the injured ankle. "You can't play anymore today, that's certain. Don't worry, Bobby, I'll get you back next week for the Academy game. Here, Tommy, you and Roy help him back to the bus. No, no, you cannot go back in; I don't care how it feels.

You've had your ankle twisted, I'll tape it after we get home. Take his shoe off and help him to the bus, boys." The yellow bus which had brought them down was waiting in the drive behind the outfield. The coach looked round for a sub. His second string catcher?

"Hey, Coach, I'll take over first if you want."

"You? Ever play first before?"

"Yessir. Once at the Academy I did when our regular man was sick with flu."

"Ok. You take first, Ronny. Let's see now; George, suppose you go in at second. All right now, boys, forget all that. Only one more inning. How you feel, Jim?" The big pitcher was yanking on a windbreaker he always wore on the bench.

"Me? I've got one more good inning left, Coach."

"Ok, I'll string along with you. I'm gonna stay with you, Jim. Now come on, boys; let's see if we can't get a bigger lead to make things easy for Jim."

But Abraham Lincoln went out in order and they came to the last of the ninth with that one run bigger than ever.

Only three more outs; three more outs, Jim, three more outs, Mike, three more outs and we'll go against the Academy an unbeaten team. If we can lick this pitcher, we'll sure show that boy Heywood something, too. Only three more outs, thought Ronny, as the infield burned the ball across to him and Mike Fronzak shot one at him from the plate. Three more outs.

"C'mon now, guys; c'mon, Jim, stay in there, Jim, every minute . . ."

Aw, shoot!

The first batter leaned back to avoid a high inside one. The ball hit his bat and looped over third base in safe ground near the foul line. Shoot! Only good fielding prevented the runner from stretching it into a double.

Now the Bannister bench was up and yelling. Last of the ninth, one run behind, nobody out, and a man on first.

"Throw it and duck, big boy. Throw it and duck up there." Jim stood in his familiar pose, not hearing their comments, cool and undisturbed. He stepped to the rubber and quickly shot in the pitch.

"Strike one!" The clatter and clamor from the opposing bench died suddenly away. Instead, their own confident noise rose over the diamond. Jim still had his stuff. Jim was as good as ever.

"Atta boy, Jim! 'At's pitching!'"

"Nice and loose now, Jim, boy . . ."

"You're the baby, Jim . . ."

"Stay in there, Jim, every minute, Jim . . ."

The batter hit. A slow, looping ball which lofted over Ronny's head and spun smack on the right field chalkline like a boy's top. Aw, nuts! There's luck for you! Eight innings of perfect pitches, a couple of bloopers, a couple of fluke hits and there you are, bang goes your ball game. Chester came racing in from right and was fortunate to get the ball in time to hold the runner on third. Shoot! Third and first, nobody down. This is bad, this is sure bad.

Now the Bannister bench and the crowded stands behind were wild with excitement. The clatter and noise and shouting increased when the runner on first ambled down to second on Jim's first pitch. Mike, behind the plate, made no play on him. From the bench the coach was shouting, his hands around his mouth. Ronald heard nothing. Then he saw. He was beckoning, beckoning the whole infield in closer on the grass.

Ronald came in slowly, while the batter took a toehold and the stands shrieked at him.

"Step in front of it, Tommy."

"Hey, Tommy, thizza one you want . . ."

"This the big one, Tommy-boy; a hit means a run, anything goes . . ."

Tommy hit. Ronald saw the ball passing, a line drive between where he stood and second base. He made a desperate dive with his gloved hand, speared it, stumbled, fell, and the ball rolled away on the grass.

The field was confusion. Everyone was running. Then over all the uproar he heard Jim's cool tones from the box.

"Home, Ronny, home, home!"

Ronald didn't need to be told. He knew they were all going as hard as they could, giving everything they had. Picking himself up he lunged for the ball, grabbed it, and burned it in to the plate. Mike slapped it hard on the sliding runner and whipped it back to third where the other Bannister runner was bearing down. Mancini had to get down for the throw, somehow he held it, and put it on the man at his feet. Two out! Two out and a man on first.

Instantly everything changed. What had been a sure rally died away, killed at its most promising moment. The noise from the Bannister bench became perfunctory, the cheers and shrieks from the low bleachers behind were silenced, the clamor died down; now the sounds came from their own side, from the coach pleading with them to hold it, his two fists upraised, from the subs yelling at them to get the next batter, from the men around the infield, and the boys out there behind.

"Cool and nervous, Jim . . ."

"Now let's go, Jim . . ."

"Ok, Jim, nice and loose, Jim."

"That's pitching, Jim."

"Let him hit it, Jim; we'll pick it up for you."

He did hit, a grass cutter toward first. Ronald felt nervous. He got down on one knee to make it sure. He wanted to make it safe, and watched the rasping hard grounder come at him. It struck his glove, bounced up in the air, and in his excitement he stabbed at the ball and missed. There it was, on the ground, rolling away from him. He pounced on it, pulled himself to his feet and dashed for the bag. By a second he managed to cross over before the runner.

They tramped happily across the thick grass of the outfield toward Bob Patterson and the waiting bus, toward the gym and the showers at Abraham Lincoln, toward their clothes and dinner. Jim, his windbreaker slung over his shoulders, his red hair damp and moist, was grinning; Mike Fronzak was still carrying his catcher's mask, and Ned was spitting into his glove, a smile on his face. Crane Davis, the manager, with the bat bag, and the coach came up in the rear. Everyone was shouting something.

"Hey there, Ronny . . ."

"That's playing, Ronny . . ."

"Shucks, it's your pitching, Jim . . ."

"No, sir! You saved that game."

"Boy, were you hot, Ronny!"

"We were all hot today."

"Yeah, whoops, bring on that pitcher up there on the Hill."

"Let's go, gang, let's go."

"Let's get that Academy crowd, gang."

They piled into the yellow bus. Bob Patterson with his ankle on a seat was smoking a cigarette. He quickly put it out as the crowd piled in. At the Academy no one would have dared smoke in training. Ronald suddenly looked round at their dirty stained uniforms, some of the kids wearing faded sweaters, or sweatshirts underneath, all of them so different from the spick and span team on the Hill. They were different, this crowd. They were different, but they could play ball.

And they were a great bunch to play with. He felt affection for them, for Jim, tired and drawn about the mouth, for Bob, wincing as the bus moved forward with a jerk, for Mike, slumped in his seat in the rear. For all the rest, laughing and yelling at each other, calling back and forth, to Mac the driver, to the coach. His face was as wet and sweaty as theirs. It was easy to see what he had gone through on the bench that final inning.

The bus moved on. For just a minute their jokes and shouts were lost as the gears ground. Then they rolled down the highway. "Hey, Coach!" Someone from the rear was yelling at him. "Hey, Coach. If this Ronny is as good next fall as he is at baseball, we're gonna have a team 'at won't lose a game."

The coach frowned. That was one of his superstitions. He never permitted cracks about games to come. He pretended not to hear and said something to the driver. Then he leaned over to Ronald in the next seat.

"You sure kept your head on that ball, Ronald. You played that one just right."

Now for the Academy. Say, we'll show that crowd something.

III

A feeling of uneasiness hung over the entire room. Chairs squeaked continually, making a chorus of scratchy noises. Voices hummed and buzzed. It was the end of the marking period; the day that came regularly once every few months. And it was the last hour of the day—when in every homeroom each student's report card was issued for the period.

This scene, so different from anything at the Academy, always interested Ronny. At the Academy you did your work everyday or else you got a detention and stayed in afternoons until you did. Here you might fail in a subject and not be sure of having failed until the end of the marking period. He looked around the excited class, at the boys in sweaters without neckties or coats, now all familiar figures who had names and personalities attached. At the girls who gave the room that high-pitched tone so strange to him from the start. At Stacey in a kind of shirt with sleeves cut high above the elbows and the school name in green on his breast; at Ned LeRoy,

156

slumped in his seat and staring ahead, apparently prepared for the worst; at Meyer Goldman in the back of the room, laughing nervously with Mike Fronzak across the aisle. And at Sandra in front. Especially at Sandra. She had on the white shoes with brown tips, and the pink sweater. . . .

Tap-tap. Tap-tap-tap. Mr. Kates standing by his desk tapped severely with his pencil for order. He glanced over the crowded room. "Quiet, please, quiet. Keep it down." For about a minute he stood silently waiting, glancing around the forty seats, every one occupied by a nervous boy or girl. All save one. Gordon Brewster at the side was undisturbed by the sight of the report cards in Mr. Kates' hand. The noise, the chatter, the squeaking of chairs subsided. Slowly the teacher came forward with that little brown package in his fist.

Eager hands reached out. Subdued murmurs of delight or deep silence even more meaningful greeted the cards. He came down the aisle toward Ronald. As he slipped the card down on the desk, he leaned over, whispering, "Will you please step into Mr. Curry's office a minute before you leave, Ronald?"

He knew at once. He knew without opening

the small folded card what had happened. He had failed. But he didn't know the whole of it.

At the top of the folded brown cardboard were the words: REPORT CARD. Underneath that, one line: ACCOMPLISHED IN STUDIES. Every pupil had a serial number. His serial number, 1166, was in the upper left-hand corner.

The card was ruled off into squares, one for each week in the marking period. Grades were listed at the side: 95 was high honors, 85 was honors, 70 was passing. At the top were printed the five subjects he took, and checks had been made in red ink in each square. Thus you—not to mention your teachers and your parents who had to sign the card—could see the progress or lack of it in every subject you took from week to week.

Yes, he knew. He knew all right. He knew as he studied the card that he was below 70 in Latin. But the history, that's bad. Oh, that's bad; definitely, as Sandra would say. Honors in algebra, English, and French. But the Latin and the history. That's bad. No wonder Mr. Curry wanted to see him. Ronald folded up the card and stuffed it into his pocket, discovering with some relief he wasn't in the least terrified at the coming interview as he had been whenever the

Duke called him in. Still and all, you couldn't help being a little worried.

"Come in. Sit down, Ronald." Mr. Curry was telephoning, but he put one hand over the mouthpiece and nodded toward a chair. Then he went on talking. "Yes. Yes, I think so. I imagine he will. Yes, I'd agree to that. At the next meeting of the Board? All right. Yes, I will. Yes, if you wish. All right. Very good. Call me Tuesday then. All right. Good-bye."

While he was talking, Ronald watched him. You'd certainly never think he was the principal of a big high school. Rather a colorless man, on the whole. Naturally you weren't exactly terrified when he called you into his office. Still and all, you couldn't help feeling a little worried.

"Ronald, sit down. Glad to see you. This is almost the first chance I've had to talk to you since you got out of the hospital. Everything working out?"

Surprising man. You got ready for a kind of a bawling out, and then you got a question like that. "Uhuh. Yessir."

"I see. That little incident was unpleasant for you; but it sort of cleared the atmosphere, didn't it?"

"Yessir. It sure did."

He smiled. "Let's see now. You've been here four, no five months nearly, haven't you? Tell me, how do you like us on the whole? Do you like this school?"

"Yessir, I like it. I like it now."

"H'm. I imagine it must have been hard for you at first. Different from the Academy." He looked down at the ruler in his hand. He glanced at the papers on his desk and rearranged them. He looked over at the window with the shade half pulled. But he never looked straight at you the way the Duke did. "H'm. Tell me, Ronald, what do you think of your report card this period?"

The question startled him. "Not so hot."

"No, it wasn't, was it? What seems to be the matter?"

"I really don't know, sir."

"Study habits? You surely don't need to be told how to study. You've been taught that already. We've had several boys from the Academy; they all had first rate study habits."

"Yessir, I mean, nosir."

"Now it's probably true, you had more individual attention in your work at the Academy." Ronald found himself breaking in to explain how things were.

"See, at the Academy you had to do your homework because you had a two-hour study period in Hall every night."

"Exactly. Here you have no study hall at night. You can go to the movies. Or listen to the Aldrich Family or see your girl. Here you're on your own. We can't watch you, we can't baby you. We don't want to. In this school, Ronald, every pupil has to be responsible for himself. That's one of the principles of a democracy, isn't it?"

Well, yes. Yes, he had something there. Obviously this diffident man, so unlike the Duke, had much more on the ball than you'd think at first glance. He wasn't a personality. Yet . . .

"Now there's one thing you've got to learn, everyone here has to learn. In this school you're on your own. *You* are lucky. You don't need to be taught how to study. You've been taught that. But in a democracy each citizen is on his own. It's up to him. You must get used to being on your own and you better do so here, now."

"Yessir." He understood. The man behind the desk leaned back, his hands behind his head, and looked at the shaded window.

"You know, it's a funny thing, I remember you so well last fall in that football game. You were a fine player, and I hope you'll be just as good on our team next year. You were a great little fighter out there, that's why you licked us."

Well, maybe so. Not exactly. But then, yes, maybe.

The principal paused a minute. "I can remember once in that last quarter watching you go through our line—and our line was plenty tough last fall—with Stacey and Goldman on your neck and . . ."

Suddenly he was back. Back on Academy field, and his cleats were digging into the turf, and his heart was pounding, and clutching hands were grabbing at him, and he could hear Goldman's tense breathing in his ear . . . "huff . . . huff . . . huff . . ."

". . . and that's the way you must be in your work, too. You've got to be aggressive, you've got to lick your studies. Or they'll lick you. Have you been really fighting your studies this way in the last six weeks?"

From a feeling of warmth and satisfaction, from the field behind the Academy he came back to earth and the principal's room at Abraham Lincoln High. With him came an uneasy feeling of what was coming. Ronald's respect for this quiet man grew. Nope, he wasn't a personality like the Duke. His clothes, for instance, weren't at all like the Duke's, and somehow he didn't wear them the same way. But he had something.

"Nosir."

"Have you been neglecting your work at all the last few weeks, do you think?"

"Nosir, yessir, maybe . . ."

"What for?" Ronald was now bewildered. This man was amazing the way he pinned you down to things, the way he got things out of you.

"Do you think possibly you haven't been working as much nights as you should?"

"Yessir, possibly."

"Well, what have you been spending your time on? Girls?"

"Yessir, I mean nosir, I mean, maybe so."

"Any one girl?"

"Yessir."

"It wouldn't be Sandra Fuller, would it?"

There! It was out now. The principal was tapping the ruler gently on the desk and looking down hard at it. Ronny felt warm all over, and he knew red was coming up into his face. But the man behind the desk still stared at the ruler.

"Sandra's a lovely girl. I don't blame you for

liking her. Been seeing a good deal of her, do you think, lately?"

"Yessir."

"How much, since you came out of the hospital?"

"Two, three times a week."

"Or more?"

Hang it, this man had something, he really had something. "Yessir, I guess . . . well, maybe."

"I guess so, too." He laughed. Ronald laughed. This made things easier. "Yes, I guess so, too. Tell you why; reason is I've seen you twice in the last month at the Empire with her, and several times in at Walgren's drinking cokes. Right?"

"Yessir."

"Now see here, Ronald. Sandra's a fine girl. She's a swell kid. But just think a minute. You know, I can remember when your father was in Yale, and I remember seeing him play in the game in the Bowl in '22, was it? No, '23. The one when he ran way out to the side and grabbed the lateral pass in the last minute of play. Right down the field for a touchdown. What a game that was! A heartbreaker for us to lose. When I watched you on the field last fall I could see your dad every minute; same way of holding your head, of handling the ball, of waiting until the last minute to chuck a pass. Look! That's what you're risking, all that. Yale, that's your job. Just imagine how your dad would feel if you failed to get into Yale. Imagine!"

He leaned over, and for the first time looked Ronald squarely in the face. "You could, you know, if you keep on this way!" Then quickly he leaned back and began turning the ruler over and over in his hands, and staring down at it silently.

Well, there really wasn't much you could say to this sort of thing. He hadn't thought of it that way, never.

"I'm mighty glad you like Sandra. She's one of the finest girls in this school. I'm glad you like us; we like you. You're part of the school, you're one of us. It's true, I know, you had a hard time at first; the boys were a little tough on you. Because you came from the Academy they suspected you, they had to get to know you. There's cruelty here. It's a kind of primitive cruelty that's hidden away in us all, I guess. We try to keep it down, yet every once in a while it does crop out, and you happened, as I say, to be the victim. But that's over. We all like you and respect you and want you to like us. And we want you to do well here. Only you must do your part. You've got to think first of all of getting into Yale."

"Yessir."

"Just imagine how you'd feel a year from now, how Sandra would look at you if you failed your College Boards. If you want to see Sandra, that's fine. See her weekends and see her then as much as you like. But keep your evenings all week for work. You had baseball in the afternoon, and you just weren't doing the work. From Monday to Friday, remember, you have a full time job on your hands. Getting into Yale."

"Yessir."

"Don't forget, I can't study for you; neither can your parents or your teachers. You're old enough now to be on your own. You're a citizen of a democracy. You have responsibilities. See you live up to them."

He stood up. He held out his hand. He looked you in the face, just the trace of a smile on his lips.

"Yessir, I will. You bet I will, Mr. Curry." They shook hands, a firm, hard fist. Ronny liked him, liked everything about him. 'Course, he wasn't a personality as the Duke was. But just the same, he was some gent.

"Oh! One thing more." Ronald turned at the doorway. "Naturally you're ineligible to play baseball until your marks come up in the next period. You understand, that means no more extramural sport this year."

He stumbled from the room. He hardly saw the girls typing away behind the counter in the big room outside. He moved into the corridor, bewildered. He was dizzy. No more extramural sport! He couldn't play on the baseball team!

Jeepers! That meant he couldn't play next week against the Academy!

IV

"Hey, Ronny."

"Hullo there! What's up?"

"How 'bout the flickers tonight?"

"Can't do it."

"Why not?"

"'Cause I gotta work."

"Work?"

"Sure. Work."

"Aw, c'mon. Cagney and Joan Fontaine."

"Nope. I made a rule I just wouldn't go out again nights until I got my marks back."

So it was work. Work every evening in the week. Latin. History. Other things, too.

"Look, Ronny! Hey, Ronald Perry, have you got your tickets for the Junior Prom next week?"

"Nope. Can't make it, Jane."

"But you must. We all want you to come. Why a couple of seasoned rug cutters like Sandra and you . . ."

"I know. But I gotta study. I made a rule with myself. . . ."

"Oh, you *must* come. Casey's band. It'll be snazzy."

"Sorry. I'd like to. But I just can't."

"Look, if you change your mind will you buy your tickets off me, please?"

"I will, sure I will; only you better not count. I really hafta work these nights."

It was work. Work every night in the week. Latin. History. Other things, too.

"Ruth, what's the matter with Ronald and that girl these days?"

"What girl, Dad?"

"That girl he used to be seeing every evening.

Fred Fuller's daughter, what's her name? He used to be over there almost every night."

"Well, I guess he's worried about his work. It shocked him being kept out of the baseball game against the Academy although he hasn't said much. But it was a big disappointment to him, I know. He's made a rule with himself he won't go anywhere at night during the week until he's raised his marks. So far this period he's stuck to it."

"Fine! Good enough. I noticed he's upstairs almost every night recently. Do you imagine he's really studying though, or listening to the Aldrich Family? Well, his marks will tell the story soon enough."

For it was work. Work every night. Latin. History. Other things, too.

"Oh, Ronald. Been looking everywhere for you. Buy your tickets offa me, will ya?"

"Tickets? What for?"

"Senior Play next week."

"Nope. Can't make it."

"Sure you can. You'll have to go. Why, it'll be super."

"No, Jerry, honest I can't. I must work tomorrow night."

"Work!"

"Uhuh, work."

"What's the idea? You better be careful or you'll make the National Honor Society. Is that what you're after?"

"No, all I'm after is, can I make the football team and play next fall against the Academy. See?"

So it was work. Work every night. Latin. History. English. Other things, too.

June came; warm, soft nights when you wanted to be anywhere except at a desk with a French book or a Cicero or a Muzzey's *History of the United States*. It was the next to last week in school. It was the end of the period. The same noises, the same clatter, the same squeaking of chairs as Mr. Kates stood there again with the report cards in his hand.

Tap-tap. Tap-tap-tap. Standing beside his desk he glanced over the crowded room and tapped for order. "Quiet please, quiet. Keep it down." For a minute he watched the forty seats, each occupied by a nervous boy or girl—one, Ronald's—by an extremely worried boy.

Gee, if I don't pick up, if I don't do well this period, I maybe won't get to play against the

Academy next fall. Not playing in the baseball game was bad, that was bad all right. But if I don't get to play in the football game! Why then most prob'ly I wouldn't get to Yale, either.

Mr. Kates came slowly down the aisle by the window. Eager hands reached out. Subdued murmurs of delight or deep silence even more meaningful greeted the cards. He walked down the second aisle toward Ronald.

Gee, if I don't pick up this period, I won't be able to play against the Academy. I wish now I'd worked weekends, too. I did work Friday nights. I wish I'd worked Saturdays and Sundays. I maybe won't make the football team.

He came a step nearer. Then he leaned over, whispering, "Will you please step into Mr. Curry's office a minute before you leave today, Ronald?"

Jeepers! There it was! No football team. No Yale. Disgrace!

Sweat came out on his forehead. He was suddenly warm all over.

After that work, after that studying, too. I certainly wish I'd worked Saturdays and Sundays, I sure wish I had.

He took the small folded card in his hand and

opened it; but his eyes were blurred and he couldn't read it. Naturally not, it was upside down. Then Jim, half-turned in his seat, looked at it and spoke.

"Boy! Boy, are you hot, Ronny!"

Mr. Kates came back down the aisle. He leaned over again and whispered, "You see what you can do if you really try, Ronald."

"Yessir." He looked at the report card again, this time reading it. 95 in Latin and History. In the others he was 85.

Half an hour later Mr. Curry was greeting him with that look which might mean a whole lot or nothing at all. "Come in. Come in, Ronald. I shan't keep you a minute." His tone was not pleased, his face as immovable as ever. He looked at the window shade, at the ruler in his hands. You couldn't tell what this man was thinking.

"You've got your report card for this period, haven't you? Well, now you see what you can do if you really try, Ronald."

Older folks were like that. They weren't very original. In the evening after dinner his father called to him as he came downstairs to go out.

"Ronald! I've just signed your report card for

the last period. Glad to see that pick up. It's better."

"Yessir, it's better."

"You see now what you can do if you really try, don't you?"

Migosh! That's the third one. Well, if Dad felt so good about it, this was the moment to ask for the car.

"Uhuh. Say, Dad, can I have the car tonight, can I?"

His father laughed out loud. A good sign. "Yes, I guess you can tonight. But see here now. I want you to keep this record up next year, understand. No sloping off when football starts. You've shown us what you can do when you really try."

Yippee! Yowser! Now for that football team and the Academy game. He drove across town to the Fuller house at the corner under the bright light where Jim had passed him that night in the Ford with the signs painted on it. Sandra was on the porch. She came down the steps as he stopped. She got into the car.

"Yowser! D'ja hear what I got in the last period marking?"

"I hear you did better than all right."

"Sure did. Two 95's and the rest 85."

"Oh, Ronald! How wonderful! Then you can play football next fall."

"You bet. If I can make the team."

"Make the team! Well, now you see what you can do if you really try, don't you?"

6

Once all this had been strange and confusing. Once it had been bewildering; the women teachers, the swarms of kids everywhere, the strange faces, the books you got for nothing instead of buying yourself. Even the books stamped in red on the edges, "Property of the Senior High School," had been strange. The books with slips pasted inside the front cover reading, "This is the property of the City. Any pupil defacing or losing this book will be required to replace it with a new one."

Now all this was familiar. Rooms were rooms he knew and had lived in, the teachers were men and women he liked or disliked, the boys and girls were no longer a mass of strange, unaccustomed faces. The rush and confusion of registration seemed normal. The kids he met in the hallways and the various classrooms were now his friends.

"Hullo, Tom; hullo, Jane; hullo, Ruth. You in Mr. Kates' homeroom this year? So'm I. Hullo, Dave; hullo, Meyer; glad to see you, Meyer. Howsa old whip, Meyer? Hullo, George; hullo, Grace. Nope, got to get my locker number, Bill; justa minute and I'll be with you. Say, there's some new boys in class and some new girls, too. Hullo, Steve; hullo, Dan. Why, there's Ned LeRoy. Hullo, Ned, how are ya, Ned?"

All this was familiar now—the rooms, the corridors with the murals of sport on the walls, the stairways, crowded and jammed between classes, the cafeteria on the third floor, the faces of the boys and girls.

"How do, Mr. Kates. Yes, Mr. Kates. I hope so, Mr. Kates, if I'm good enough to make the team. Yes, I'll try to keep my marks up like they were the end of last year; yessir, I will, I surely will. Hullo there, Stanley; hullo, Barbara; hullo, Don; hullo, Jim. Why, Jim, how are ya? You betcha, Jim, you betcha! Yeah, he's a new boy. Mr. Kates introduced him to the class in our homeroom period. Looks like he might be good backfield material."

During the day Ronald arranged his program. English in 209 under Mrs. Fisk. Physics in 322 under Mr. Vickery. History in his homeroom under Mr. Kates. Virgil in 215 under Mrs. Taylor. French in 304 under Mr. Leonard.

Then it was time to eat. Sitting again at a table in that familiar hall with boys and girls he knew, a thought suddenly struck him. For the first time he didn't feel a stranger. He was really a part of Abraham Lincoln High. He was used to all this, to the chattering girls, to the noise, the giggling, to the differences between the two schools. Which made him realize that he had spent the whole day without comparing everything with the Academy as he used to do.

Later on, however, he had plenty of chances to compare them. Dressed in shorts and a thin undershirt with football socks and shoes on, he stood in the warm September sunshine with his arms around Meyer and Jim, his friends. The squad made a semicircle on the rich turf, the coach in the center nervously passing a football from one hand to the other. He was different from Baldy, very different from Baldy as Ronald was to discover. That afternoon he wore his baseball uniform with the cap down over his eyes, looking more than ever the professional baseball player; competent, keen, sure of himself and his ability. Silence came over the chattering group.

"For you new men . . . we have one or two transfers this fall . . . and also for the sophomores on the squad, I want to start the season by saying this: if you don't mean business, turn in your suit. If you don't intend to keep training, turn in your suit right away. Football's a game that's tough enough when a man's fit, and it's not a game for anyone who won't train. If you can't take it and hand it out, too, turn in your suit. Here at Abraham Lincoln we don't like moral victories. We play hard, we play to win, we like to win. We can't win all the time; but we hope to win our share. We mean business.

" 'Nother thing, I want you to concentrate every day on the work of that day. Don't want anyone thinking about a possible Intersectional game sometime next winter. Now here in this school we use what is called the T-formation. We use the T-formation with the man in motion. The name T-formation is wrong. Actually this style involves fifty formations, and we use twenty. This end spreads, this end drops, and so forth. I call it the T-formation because everyone else does. Tomorrow I'll explain it carefully on the blackboard for the newcomers.

"At first you won't like it, some of you. It'll seem strange until you get used to it, this formation with a man in motion. It isn't really novel, in fact it starts from a formation that's basic to football as developed back in Walter Camp's day. The real secret lies in the use of the man in motion. This is the thing that helps the offense by confusing the defense. Why does it mix up the defense? Simply because it blends the flanker attack with a hard, fast-hitting, quick-opening attack. Through the various changes in formational structures it places a terrific burden on the defense.

"Naturally a formation of this kind demands letter-perfect execution by the offensive side. It means every single player and every sub, too, must know his assignments down to the smallest detail. There's no room for sloppiness. There's lots to learn and not much time to learn it in. Some coaches say high school boys aren't smart enough to grasp the essentials of the T-formation. I believe they are. Think I've proved it by our record here, too. But it means work, hard work, lots of hard work everyday. We have no time for horseplay and fooling. Once more, if you don't mean business, turn in your suit to Mr. Coughlin—right now.

"The objects of football are simple. First, you must know what to do. Second, how to do it. The signals tell you what to do. The question of how to do it is up to the men on the field themselves. We teach them the idea; but they must use their originality in applying what they are taught."

He stopped suddenly and glared at them round the circle. There was a pause. No one spoke.

"Ok, let's go."

As September wore on and the opening game drew near, Ronny was astonished to discover that the coaching at Abraham Lincoln was really more intensive and perhaps even better than at the Academy. Baldy was a math teacher and a crackerjack; his record in College Board Examinations was as good as that of any teacher in the Academy. He was a fine football coach and could turn out winning teams; but he was a fine football coach secondarily. He was a better teacher. Whereas at Abraham Lincoln the coach taught nothing. His official title was Athletic Director. This fooled no one. Because he was first of all the coach. As such he knew his stuff.

For this guy was a scrapper. He was a scrapper all right. He had played in a very different—and a tougher—league than Baldy's. Ronny liked Baldy as a man, as a human being, as a friend; but in the weeks of practice that followed under a burning September sun, he had to admit this man understood football. You really had to know the game to coach the T-formation with a man in motion. And the player, you yourself, had to work to learn it, to execute it, to start on the right number, to feel the principles of balanced line blocking, most of all to get the time element involved with the man in motion.

You couldn't play under Baldy and not know something about football. Yet much of this was fresh to Ronald, and all of it was difficult at first. True, the tackling dummy he was used to. The bucking strap. The charging machine. The practice, the almost endless practice in blocking, too, even though the coach insisted on longer sessions with the machines than he had ever endured. But the eternal drill, drill, drill was tedious and fatiguing. It was drudgery of a kind he had never before experienced. No use talking, football was more fun at the Academy.

New also were some of the difficulties met in the high school brand. At the Academy Steve Ketchum had to work for his scholarship; so did Dave Freeman. Occasionally they were late at the field for practice because of lab work, and certainly waiting on table after a hard practice in the afternoon was far from easy. But many of the players at Abraham Lincoln had jobs, too. They were plenty busy, in school and out. Don Westcott, the center, for instance, was president of the Student Council, led the Glee Club, played football, and worked nights as an usher at the Empire. Moreover the boys all kept strict training at the Academy. They had to. Here they went home and did what they pleased at night.

So naturally the coach was obliged to be tough. He was. Ronald discovered this before their first game when the lineups were read out, and he found to his surprise he was not starting. It was the first time since his Second Form year at the

Academy he hadn't been in the opening line-up. This was a shock. So were the remarks of the coach as they were about to take the field.

"This is an easy game, you fellows, but I expect everyone to go out there just as if we were against Stainesville. Some of you new men may be surprised to find you aren't starting. Wanna say, here we don't take you on your reputation. You've gotta prove you're good first of all, you've gotta prove it the hard way same as everyone else. You know you're good all right, your families know you're good, your girl knows you're good; but you must show us. You gotta earn your place on this team by your play here, now, today; not by what you did last year.

"All right! Get out there, team. Lemme see what you've got."

•

Consequently Ronald found himself watching instead of starting that game, and others, too. They came up to the important meeting with Broadwood High undefeated.

If we can beat Broadwood today, we'll only have Stainesville and the Academy left for an undefeated season. Some of the kids said if we licked Stainesville we might even be asked to play Intersectional. Especially if we should end up by beating the Academy. Because if we beat the Academy we'll be the best team in the State, no mistake. But they'll be tough, those babies, they sure will. On account of me they'll be all out to trim us. And we'll be kinda tough, too, maybe.

During the first half and part of the second Ronald sat on the bench beside the coach.

"Fairchild, you'll start today at quarter; Perry, I want you to sit beside me," said the coach in the lockers.

So Ronny stayed on the sidelines, watching Stan Fairchild run the team. As he watched, Ronny realized that running a team from a T-formation was no cinch. There were plenty of mistakes a quarter could make, and if Stanley made some, he could have made more. In fact as they went along into the third quarter without any score, Ronald found himself just as pleased he hadn't started the game. Far too much depended on it.

None of Stan's errors escaped the eyes of the coach, who through much of the play was dictating to Gordon Brewster at his side. "Shoot! Why doesn't he watch that left half coming up?

That defensive halfback is leaving that spot wide open for our 67 pass.

"There! There goes 99 into the middle. That's all right; I'd have picked that play. Third and five.

"Hullo . . . he's passing! It's 69 on the weak side. There goes their right half; he's got it . . . no, he just knocked it down. Stan was rushed then; well, it wasn't the play to use, anyhow. And Dave should have dropped back and out to protect, the way he's been taught. Fourth and five; he's got to kick, got to."

The kick was a long spiral down the field. The coach settled back for a minute and turned to Ronald. "See what I'm trying to tell these boys? The element of surprise is what wins games. Pass when they expect a run and run when they're watching for your pass. And don't forget the quick-kick, either. The quick-kick's one of the greatest weapons you've got; it can change a whole game.

"Hey there! Hey, Stan, watch out! Look out, Stan!"

As he had been speaking the teams lined up, with their opponents in the usual single-wing formation, the ball on the 30-yard line. Stan, in safety position, was only about 20 yards back. The ball went to the tailback five yards behind the line of scrimmage, and the interference started toward the right as if for a normal running play. Only the left half didn't run. He took one step forward and quickly kicked the ball. It sailed over Stan's head, bumped and bounded along until it came to a rest on the 25-yard line. The team were now well back in their own territory.

"Shoot! Just what I was saying." Ronald recalled once long before, playing at the Academy, he had been caught the same way and hoped fervently he wouldn't have been caught this time. "Remember," said the coach. "Remember what I was telling you; remember only last Wednesday how we worked on that quick-kick? Remember, I told you it was a good play, especially with the wind at your back. Well, most likely they had the same kind of session, only they remembered. Now look where we are; back in our own territory where we can't afford to take any chances.

"What's that? Why, sure; you're quite right, Ronny; Stacey should have been able to spot that play and yelled. D'ja notice their tackle edge out on him when they lined up? Good boy. He wanted to get down fast to cover. That should have been the tip. Stan better kick on second down this time; we'll lose plenty on the exchange, plenty. But if he waits until third down, they'll know a kick is coming . . . it's the element of surprise that wins football games."

Ronny ventured a question. "How about our pass down the middle right now, Coach, our 48? Wouldn't that cross 'em up? They're certainly not expecting it."

"You're right they aren't expecting it. But in this zone, with the score so close, it's dangerous. If we were trailing by a touchdown, it might be ok. If we were behind two touchdowns, yes, definitely, that would be the play. But an interception right here would put them in a scoring position. One of the things you quarterbacks must learn is when to take chances and when not to. Right now the thing to do is to get out of this hole without giving them a scoring chance."

On the first play, Fairchild faked to the right halfback, who went tearing outside tackle without the ball, his arm crooked and his body slightly hunched over as if carrying it. Meanwhile the left halfback, actually tucking the ball under his arm, went through a quick-opening hole for four yards.

Second down, six. Fairchild went into kick formation. Standing on his own 18-yard line, he got away another good kick, low, as it should have been into the wind, and away from the safety man. It took a lucky bounce and bobbled out of bounds on their 40-yard stripe.

"Nice kick," said the coach. "We're out of that hole for the moment. I don't know whether Fairchild was aiming for the sidelines or not; but I want you boys to remember that sideline can be an awful big help sometimes. Especially if the other team has a safety man who can run back kicks. We'll put some time in on that this next week.

"Now let's see if we can get hold of that ball. The line's charging pretty well . . . all except Jake. Ronny! Tell Meyer to warm up, and get him in there. He goes across that scrimmage line fast, and a recovered fumble or a blocked kick would help a lot now."

Ronny ran down to the end of the bench, and Meyer came jogging up and bent down in front of the coach.

"Jake-boy, I want you to get in there for one reason. I want you to get across that line like a trip-hammer. I don't believe they'll try to mouse-trap you. If they do, I think you're big enough and strong enough to do a whole lot of damage anyway.

"Now look, I've noticed one thing about this boy, this passer of theirs. He's nervous, d'ja see him that last time? I've been watching him pretty close, and when he's going to pass, he wipes his right hand on his jersey . . . yep, while he's waiting for the ball. While he's waiting for it to be snapped, that's right. When he's going to run, he doesn't . . . there . . . see, see that? There's the giveaway! Watch for it and tell the other boys.

"Another thing, notice that wingback of theirs on the weak side. When there's a reverse play and he's going to hit the tackle, he'll edge up toward the line almost a foot closer than usual. There! There he goes now . . . see . . . what'd I tell you! Get it? When the play is going the other way, toward the strong side, he lines up almost a whole yard off the line of scrimmage. I've been watching him all afternoon, and you can always depend on it. Now get warmed up, and you'll be in there in a minute."

The boy blurted, "Yes, Coach," and began to jog up and down the sideline. The man on the bench turned to Ronny.

"See, Ronny, if you keep your eyes open and

189

your mind clear, you can learn lots of things about the other team. When you've found them use 'em. That's football. That's the difference between the winning team and the losing one, always."

II

It was a Saturday afternoon and Ronald decided he could treat himself to a picture, only Dad had the car playing golf. Dad always had the car. Or was about to use the car, or take the car to have it greased, or want it whenever he needed it. So Ronny, who might have called Sandra up had he been able to get the car, decided to go down alone on his bike.

At North Main he was held up by a traffic light. After it went green the cop stationed there still held them to let a long line of people move across. Some of them carried handbags. Above the noise of motors shifting gears, Ronny heard strains of music in the distance.

He sat with one foot on the curb. "Hey, kid," he asked a boy running along the sidewalk, "where's the fire?"

"The station!" The kid turned his head and

yelled back. "The station. They're leaving on the five-forty." Ronald didn't understand at all. Then the music became louder and louder, and at last a band was visible. Why, it's the High School band! He had always wondered what use a high school band was except to play at football games. Now he wondered more than ever.

As the band passed, the grins from the windows of parked cars were widespread, and the derisive remarks from the kids on the sidewalks echoed his own feelings. At the head was Vera Clark, the drum major, wearing an absurdly tall white shako with a small green plume on it. She was having great trouble with her headgear because of the wind. First the shako slanted to one side of her head and then the other. White boots came halfway up to her knees, and she wore a white skirt and a thinlooking greenish jacket.

All the girls wore green jackets and sheer white skirts which fluttered in the wind; the boys had on green peaked caps, green blazers, and thin white trousers. A good costume for the Fourth of July or even for the Academy game. But not that day. That day their faces were red. They looked cold. They undoubtedly were cold, and the uneven sounds from their instruments betrayed their feelings plainly. One small, pale boy whom Ronny had seen around the corridors at school stuck his clarinet under his arm and tried to blow his nose. The clarinet dropped to the street with a clatter that sounded even above the thin pipings of the band. He stooped over to rescue it and was promptly run down by the two bass drummers who marched unseeing up his back. The crowd roared. Ronny laughed, too. Was there ever anything more useless than the High School band!

For it was all so funny; the kids in their summer pants and coats, the tottering white shako on Vera's head, the little clarinet player, and the uneven, straggling lines. Ronald followed along to see where they were going. As the head of the crowd turned into Harrison Avenue, he saw autos pouring toward the station driveway. Then he realized the whole big parking space back of the building was blocked with cars. Never seen it like this. Never.

The platforms, too, were crowded, so full you had to push and squeeze to get through. Inside a window he saw that the waiting room, a large barren place which usually contained half a dozen bored passengers, was completely jammed. Jake

Stein, the baggage master, stood beside his door, unable to work, watching. The band now silent, holding their instruments under their arms, their hands in their pockets, managed to worm their way through the mob to a position beside the tracks. They all had a curious stork-like appearance as they stood forlornly around.

Leaving his bicycle with several others against the wall, Ronny pushed into the waiting room. Instantly he realized. The men were leaving for camp. It seemed at first as if everyone in town had some relation departing. Milt Ziegler, Goldman's first cousin, was there surrounded by his family, and Meyer, too.

"Hey, Meyer."

"Hullo, Ronny." They stood watching the crowd. At one side was Ed Swift with his dad, the president of the Trust Company, and Doc Rheinstein, standing with an arm around a boy's neck. Beyond was a black-haired Italian in a leather windbreaker whom Ronny sort of remembered having seen before. He was an island in a sea of emotional relatives. His father, old, bent, needing a shave, his mother, short, fat, with a shawl over her head, and two girls, evidently his sisters, stood beside him. In the center of the room was a bunch of Negroes with their girls, all laughing and joking. They called across the packed room, shouting and kidding. Nearly everyone else, especially the older people, was solemn and quiet.

"Let's us get out of this," said Meyer. They edged their way through the crowd. There, bang in front of them, was Jim Stacey.

"Hey, guys! Say, this is something, isn't it?" The three of them together stood watching. The platform was jammed with people, everyone holding to their hat with one hand and the arm of some boy with the other. You could easily tell the ones who were leaving. They all carried small handbags. Then Ronny noticed two colored people who weren't so happy.

"Gosh, it's Ned! Ned LeRoy. Is that Ned LeRoy?" Stacey shook his head and shouted in the confusion.

"Naw, it's Tom, his brother. Looks like him, doesn't he?"

Another look made Ronald realize his mistake. Tom also had been a school football star, and he had worked since graduation in the school cafeteria. In fact Ronny had confused him with Ned one of his first days at Abraham Lincoln.

So Tom was leaving! Tom had played against the Academy the year Ronald made the team as a sub; a darn good end, too. Shutting his eyes he could see that square Negro face on the end of the line, could picture him adjusting his head-gear and waiting on his knees for the coming play. Now Tom was going to be a soldier. He was going into the army. It brought everything close to Ronny, made him feel a participant and not a spectator of what was taking place. The platform of noisy jostling people became real to him.

The colored boy's face was serious. He wasn't laughing. By his side was a good-looking, light-skinned girl without a hat. Apparently she had put on her best clothes to see him off. Edging nearer with Jim and Meyer beside him, Ronny could see she was close to Tom, right up against him, and he held her tight with one arm. In the other he carried a worn old handbag.

The crowd shoved, pushed, banged its way here, surged through there; men, women, kids, draftees, older men, a few Legionnaires in uniform. The trio stuck together, watching as a man climbed onto a baggage truck and stood with his camera pointed downward, flashing bulbs.

"Dykes. From the *Courier*," remarked Stacey. Then two older men with armbands, most likely draft board members, jammed through.

"Ray Kelley? Ray Kelley? Anybody here seen Ray Kelley?"

Several girls in bluish uniforms with packages of cigarettes worked past. They were offering them to all the boys leaving, and held out a couple to Tom. He saw neither the girls in uniform nor the cigarettes. While the crowd was shifting nervously about, he remained motionless, holding the girl to him. At the end of the platform the band started playing badly, out of tune.

Was there ever anything more useless than a high school band? Or girl drum majors? Vera, waving her baton, stopped suddenly to grab at her white shako which the wind seemed determined to carry away. Even Meyer and Jim snickered. No wonder, for she had thrown on a faded fur coat which hardly came below her knees. With her white boots this made her look more stork-like than ever.

A sharp whistle rang through the clear air.

"All right, stand back, please; stand back now, please. Up there, stand back, will you?"

A railroad official strode up and down the white line along the platform, warning the crowd and waving them back as the shriek of the distant engine came down the track. It was the custom of the train going over the grade crossing at Whistleville. Whistleville was on no map of the town. But if you said Whistleville, everyone knew what you meant. It was the section where the colored people lived.

Jim nudged him. Ronny turned and saw Tom, who was going off to be a soldier. He was kissing the girl, and she had her arms tight around his neck, so tight that his hat was tilted back from his forehead. Tom was going off to camp, this minute. He was leaving home and Whistleville. For the first time Ronald thought of Whistleville not as a part of town you avoided but as someone's home. He felt queer in his throat. It was funny when you thought of it; Whistleville, home, soldiers, Tom, that girl.

Up and down the platform the noise and confusion increased. The band was louder, their lack of harmony more evident. In the excitement those kids in green blazers with puffed-out cheeks and red hands were more ridiculous than ever. They were unnoticed and unheard as the train roared into the station, for nobody was paying the least attention to them or to the stork-like Vera, frantically waving her green and white baton, the fur coat bouncing up and down on her shoulders as she motioned with her stick.

The train thundered past down the track, the brakes creaked, and it came slowly to a stop. Above the crowd the coaches were empty. There was a movement toward the steps, and Ronny noticed the tall figure of Mr. Swift with one arm round his son, and the fat Italian woman kissing her boy; and then the little man who needed a shave had him. Gosh! He was, yessir, he was kissing him, too. The woman with the black shawl over her head moved away as the boy hopped on the steps. She was supported by a girl on each side, and followed by the little old man who was patting her shoulders. Now Ronald remembered him. It was Crispi. Old Crispi who ran the fruit store on South Main and Gardiner. That boy must have been Crispi's son.

"All right there, boys. Everybody on. All aboard, boys." They were climbing up the steps. Inside they were shoving suitcases into the racks, grinning down from the windows, waving. Ronny saw Ed Swift and Mike Haskell who used to work summers in the A & P. G'bye, Mike. Hey, Mike, g'bye. Mike couldn't hear. And there was that Polish kid who used to deliver the *Courier*. Was he really old enough to be a soldier! Meyer was shouting to someone, so was Jim on the other side.

Suddenly the cop standing beside the step of the nearest coach drew up his hand to his cap. And Mr. Swift took off his hat and placed it over his heart. So did Meyer Goldman at his side.

The Star-Spangled Banner! You could hardly hear the music, just a bar or two. That useless band; why didn't they have the Legion band or a good band?

Inside the car the men had stopped waving. Someone was singing. It was Jim. No, it was Meyer. Now more, lots and lots of people. The band was louder, you could actually hear it plainly, playing pretty well, too.

From the car inside Ed Swift was singing, and Mike Haskell, too, and Meyer on one side of him and Jim on the other and Mr. Swift and everyone around. Suddenly his eyes were moist. Darn it all, he thought, this is silly. The band blared out the last bars. They were firm, emphatic. Say! Maybe that band isn't quite so useless after all.

"All aboard!" The train gave a jerk.

Then Tom leaped down. He'd been standing on the steps of the train. He shoved the conductor aside and jumped to the platform. The girl standing beside Meyer threw herself around Tom's neck. The car was moving now.

"Hey, hey-there, Tom! You'll miss the train."

They dropped apart. He plunged back through to the steps of the car. The girl was smiling at him.

The train moved. He waved to Tom. "Good luck, Tom, you tell 'em, Tom-boy, hit 'em hard, Tom, that's the stuff, that's the old stuff." The cars vanished in the dusk at the end of the platform. He felt foolish, he was yelling at empty space.

Once more there was moisture in his eyes. Doggone, it's cold, it's awfully cold! What was he crying for? Keith and Eric and Tommy Gilmore would have roared. Certainly it was a good thing Meyer and Jim Stacey were at his elbow. It was the wind, the cold. Sure it was the wind.

But in his heart he knew it was not the cold. It was Tom LeRoy leaving his girl and it was the look on her face after the train pulled out that made tears come to his eyes.

III

When you win, when passes click, when the interference forms smoothly in front and you cut in for five, ten, twenty yards, when the sun shines and your girl's sitting up there in the High School stands and the score mounts, yes, then football's fun. That's grand, that's something like.

But this sort of thing wasn't fun; it was agony. For almost the first time since he began playing football he longed to hear the sound of the whistle.

Of all days to have it rain, the day of the Academy game, the one day we want a good dry field and firm footing! The rain pelted down his neck, oozed into his shoes, made each pad a sodden lump of lead. He looked around. The 16-yard line! One more touchdown and we'll be licked; surely, positively licked. Ruefully he remembered standing on the same spot and saying that same thing to himself before the second touchdown. And the third.

Then the whistle blew.

The team picked itself out of the mud and straggled across the mire into the gymnasium. Into the lockers and clean clothes; relief from that incessant pounding, a chance to rest, to stretch out quietly, to pull themselves together.

The familiar room was warm and dry; in one corner steam was hissing cheerfully from the pipes, and the sight of those little piles of fresh, clean clothes before every locker was comforting. They trooped in, sodden and dripping, saying nothing because there wasn't much you could say, chucking their headgears across the benches in disgust, despondent and disappointed. 19-0. What could anybody say about that kind of a score? To think this was the team that had been talked of as possibly playing an Intersectional game!

"Ok, boys." The coach brought up the rear, slamming the door on an especially severe gust of wind and rain. If he was distressed by the upset he showed no evidence of it. "Ok now, boys, get those clothes right off. Mike! Give us a hand here. Goldman, I'll fix that cut up over your eye. Doc, take a look at Jake's leg."

They hauled off their clothes, wet, soggy, disagreeable to touch, and dropped them to the floor. A small pool of water immediately collected about each pile. Mike and the Doc and the assistant coaches went around rubbing them down, repairing them for the second half. Ah, that's good. Good to be stretched out and relaxed on the hard board while Mike assailed you with the coarse, dry towel. But that score, 19-0. Gee, that's terrible, you can't laugh that off. And we were the team mentioned in the papers as going south to play Miami High. Sure, in all the newspapers!

Slowly they dressed once more. Dry socks, underwear, supporters, pads, pants, jerseys, and shoes. There. That's better. That's something like. The coach came past and slipped to the bench where Ronny was leaning over to tie his shoelaces.

"Ronald!" His voice was low. "What seems to be the trouble out there this afternoon?"

Ronny knew perfectly well what the trouble was but he didn't like to say. So he just kept leaning over his shoes. When he didn't answer, the coach continued in a low voice. "I know it's wet out there; this kind of weather hurts the T-formation the worst way. But from the bench it kinda looks as if the boys aren't together."

Nope, we surely aren't together. Of course we aren't together; how can we be together when some of the crowd are set on something beside winning a football game? That's what he wanted to say, tried almost to say as loud as he could; but it refused to come out. He mumbled something about the bad weather, the storm, the wet ball, the footing.

The coach rose. He clapped his hands. The squad gathered about, everyone's hair still wet and damp. Behind in the rear Mike passed with an armful of soaking uniforms and equipment.

"Boys, this weather is certainly tough. No use talking. I recognize what you are up against out there. The T-formation needs good firm ground to be effective. But I still feel somehow you're better'n what you've shown, and I've still got confidence in you to win, yes, even with this score. I have confidence, that is, if you'll only get going. Nineteen points a lot? Sure. But the test of a player is what he can do when he's tired. This half go out and play the kind of ball you can."

Then they were outside, out in that deluge once more. Across the way the Academy stands rose in a roar as Keith led his team at the same moment onto the field. Over the end zone was the scoreboard with those dreadful figures staring at them:

The ball was low, and from his position Ronald could watch the backs of his teammates converge on the runner, on Keith, no, on Heywood. That big halfback, heavy, powerful, fast, had been slashing holes in their line all afternoon. In the mud and slime he seemed impossible to stop, and Ronny himself had tackled him half a dozen times.

The teams lined up. Heywood took the ball once more for a sizable gain. But Ronald was noticing something else; he was watching Mike and two others break through and pile up on Keith. It was what they'd been doing ever since the kick-off. To his astonishment some of his teammates hadn't forgotten Goldman's injury of the previous season. They were still trying to pay Keith for his share in it.

There's a guy we don't like, so we'll bang him off at the start. This was their attitude. Ronny knew what they didn't seem to know, that Keith could take it. All the time they were attempting to bang him off, Steve Ketchum and Heywood had plowed through for those touchdowns.

Once again Heywood sliced into the line and

out into the secondary. He was nearly clear before he slipped and fell. That's a break, that is. On the next play they made a first down, and then Keith got loose off tackle, his most dangerous run. It was Ronny who, seeing the danger on that sloppy field, managed to knock him outside after a thirty-yard gain. He picked himself up, now as wet and soggy as he had been at the end of the first half.

"C'mon, gang, get in there, get in there and play ball like you can, will ya? Block that end, Mike, watch him every minute; get in low, Jake."

But slowly, surely, steadily, the Academy came toward their goal, toward a fourth touchdown, toward the worst licking the High School had ever taken. Keith charged in low and hard between Vic and Don Westcott who alone seemed to be holding up the center of the line, playing a magnificent defensive game. Don slapped at him and threw him off his stride as Ronny came running up. The whole play was clear before him. Keith with one arm out, stumbling in the mud; Mike and Dave rushing in hard to fall on him so that if he wasn't knocked out he'd at least know he'd been hit. It made Ronald furious. He closed in, determined not to permit them to get away with it, to block off Dave anyway. He did block him off, and as he did so Mike accidentally slipped and hit him on the chin with the full force of his fist.

He saw stars. When he came to they were standing around in the mud. Doc Roberts was leaning over, wiping his face and holding smelling salts under his nose.

"I'm ok, Doc." He rose unsteadily, feeling dizzy, tried to step out a little, managed to trot a few steps. "I'm ok." But he was not ok, and he was mad clean through. This had to end. One thing or the other. They'd have to quit and play ball—or he would.

"C'm here, gang. This way. Look. This has gotta stop. It's gotta stop or I quit. If you guys don't lay off that bird, I'll leave the field, here, right now, and I'll tell Coach why. C'mon, gang, what say, gang, let's go. Let's forget that stuff. Let's get together, let's play against that crowd there, not against each other."

"You're dead right, Ronald!" Jim Stacey, adjusting his headgear, stepped in toward the center. "Listen, you guys, lay off that fella from now on and play ball. I've been watching you, and Ronny's quite right. We've been playing against each other, not together. Let's all shoot together for the team."

"Ok, Jim."

"All right, Jim-boy."

"Sure, let's go, gang."

"Yeah, let's go."

"All right now, get in there, you guys."

The whistle blew. The teams lined up. Ronald looked around. He was standing on the 8-yard line!

It was raining harder than ever. The Academy leaned over the ball. It was snapped to Heywood, who for the first time started a fraction of a second too soon. The ball was over his shoulder, he stabbed at it, deflected it in the air. A wet figure dashed past and snatched at it in the mist. He had it. Never missing a stride he was five yards down the field before anyone turned.

"Go on, Ned, go on, Ned-boy, for Pete's sake, go on. Don't slip, Ned, go on, Ned!"

The two teams picked themselves up out of the mud and streamed along behind him, but the fleet colored boy gained with every stride.

"Yeah, team! Team, team, team. Yeah, team!" The cymbals clashed and clanged from the High

School side of the field. The first chance they had had to cheer since the kick-off.

IV

Now then, we're moving. We're really moving. For the rest of the third quarter the teams slithered up and down the center of the gridiron, both Keith and Ronald punting and handling that juicy sphere as if it were dry and easy to hold. Somehow they managed to cling to the thing.

Then toward the end of the quarter the High School team got moving. A quarterback sneak was good for a long gain. On the Academy 30-yard line, however, they were held for two plays. Third and six. They went into their huddle.

"Ok, gang. 39 on 5 count." He was winded, he puffed hard. This was Meyer's play. They went into formation.

"Hike. 27 . . . 38 . . . 40 . . . hike . . ." He leaned over, his hand on Don's wet rump. The ball came and for once the play was perfectly executed. He faked with his empty left hand to Jake, the halfback, and then in the same motion tucked the ball in Meyer's stomach, continuing back himself as if he were about to throw a pass.

Meyer roared off Roger Treadway's end into the secondary, he bounced off Steve, straightarmed Rex Heywood, and carried Keith along on his back almost five yards. The High School stands were jumping, shrieking, yelling.

Then someone shouted. Over to the left in clear territory a figure lay in the wet. Jim had gone down on the play to fake catching a possible forward and draw in one of the defensive backs in their 5-4-2 alignment. Doing so he had turned, slipped, and fallen in the open. When Ronny reached him a group of players was huddled round and he was writhing in agony on the ground.

The Doc rushed up, shoving them aside. He knelt down in a puddle, began feeling of the thigh, the leg, the calf, the ankle.

"Ouch!" Jim jerked up. "Ow . . . that hurts. . . ow . . ."

The Doc beckoned to the sidelines. "You lay still, young man. Lay still now, don't move."

Silence came over the field, and Ronny could hear them from the stands. "It's Jake . . . naw. . . it's Perry . . . no, he's up, there . . . it's Jim Stacey."

Two managers ran out with a stretcher. They rolled him over, protesting. Ronny saw he was in acute pain. On the bench Jack Train, his substitute, leaned over toward the coach. Then they were carrying Jim from the field.

The team stood disconsolately in the rain. Aw, shoot! Shucks, don't we get the breaks against us! How's that for rotten luck! First this stinking lousy weather. Then we lose our captain, the key of our passing attack, the man who was our best pass catcher.

Jack Train came running on, adjusting his dry headgear. His uniform was unsoiled, his hands were fresh and clean. Ronny looked at him almost with disgust. Heck! What good is he? Couldn't catch a dry ball at ten feet. What use is he on a day like this?

They tried a play. Then another. Something had gone, the mainspring of their nervous energy had snapped, there was no punch left. Baldy was a bear on scouting other teams, and Ronald well knew they'd been told that with Stacey out the High School's passing attack wasn't to be feared. He saw the defensive halfback in one zone slide up. Ideal for a pass if only he had a receiver.

Looking over the situation he called for a fake split buck-end run with Jake carrying the ball.

But they were waiting, and although Meyer blocked out the defensive end, the halfbacks smeared the play for a small gain. Third and nine! Shoot! Just as we were rolling, too. That's lousy luck all right. Then he heard a voice at his elbow as they went into the huddle. It was Ned, who never raised his voice, who never spoke unless you spoke to him first—Ned, who was the best defensive end in the State but never carried the ball.

"Ronny. Lemme have a look at that thing. Shoot me that flat pass up the center. I b'lieve I kin hang on to that thing."

Why not? They were stopped now. Why not have a try at it? "Ok, gang. Number 46 on 4. Got it, everyone?" He looked round at their muddy faces, heard their panting, saw their affirmative nods. "C'mon now. Formation T. 46 on 4. Hike. 27-38-40-39 . . . hike . . ." He leaned over, patting Don on his wet back. Here it comes!

Taking the ball, he turned and scuttled to the rear. Careful. Keep your balance. Watch your feet now. Both defensive halfbacks anticipating a thrust at the line had sneaked up, and Ronald, as he'd been coached, shot the flat pass over their heads into empty territory. Like lightning

Ned was there, cutting in with a swerve and taking that greasy thing in midair on the dead run. He had it! Doggone, he had it! He was off. Ronald could see nothing more, for he himself was buried under a swarm of resentful tacklers.

He didn't need to see. When he shook himself free and got the mud out of his eyes, Ned was standing beneath the goal posts and the umpire had his hands high in the air.

Another touchdown. 19-13.

You can't keep a good gang down! The band blared, squeaky noises came from the brasses, but the cheering drowned everything. Yeah, team! Team, team! Watch it, Meyer. Watch it, boy; watch that kick, it's terribly important. He remembered the coach's words as the ball was snapped back to Bob who always held it for Meyer. Give Meyer a chance, and he'll come through. He's only missed two out of the last fourteen tries.

Swell! Atta boy, Meyer, great work, Meyer. 19-14. Great work for you, too, Ned. Boy, you're hot! "C'mon now, gang, c'm here, c'm over here. Look. We got eight minutes to score. Let's get this one for Jim, gang. You bet, we'll get this one for Jim."

It was the longest eight minutes of his life. In that eight minutes he lived a hundred lives, died and was reborn a hundred times. In that space of time he suffered ages of agonies. For he was weary, beaten, his whole frame ached as it had never ached before, he seemed to be carrying around twenty pounds of heavy mud. Each step was a horrible effort. Every fall, every tackle, jarred him badly.

They kicked off, downed them close to their goal line, held them after several rushes, and got the ball near midfield.

"Ok, gang, here's our chance. Here's where we go. 48 on 3. Hip-hip. Hike." Get outa the way, Mike, get outa the way or I'll tattoo your backbone. No gain? Shoot! Third and eight to go.

He punted, poorly. But then their own line held and once more the Academy was forced to kick back. Now he gave everything he had, a delayed straight buck, a short forward to Ned which was knocked down, a forward to Bob which was incomplete. Again he had to kick.

For the third time they held despite the fierceness of the Academy attack. Dusk was descending fast in the wet and mist. You could hardly see the opposite goal posts. He called for 80. It was one of the coach's favorites, a play in which he handed the ball to Meyer who tossed it to Bob, the man in motion. His play which had been stopped three times in the first half for no gain went for twenty yards. They were creeping along, well in enemy territory now; but time was running out fast.

A fumble! A fumble! The ball slithered through the mud. He could see it, in the open. Then a figure shot toward it almost parallel to the ground. How he ever managed to hold that greasy object Ronny never knew. There he was, however, with the ball in his stomach when six men piled on top.

Ned LeRoy! Good boy, Ned! You saved us that time. Gee, that's great work, Ned, that's really super. They went into the huddle. Why not? Sure it was growing dark. Sure the ball was wet and hard to handle. But why not try it?

The defensive backs were sneaking up again, so he called for a pass down the sidelines in which the left end ran down and cut over to take the ball. Number 86 on 3. He leaned over, panting. Whew! Gosh, I'm all in. The words of the coach came suddenly to mind.

The test of a player is what he can do when he's tired.

He looked at them. Meyer on his knees in a

pool of water, Ned with his mouth open and his white teeth showing, Don hardly able to stand up, Mike with the gash in his forehead open and bleeding, everyone done in, beaten, exhausted. But the test of a player is what he can do when he's tired.

"Look, gang, let's give 'em one good one for Stacey. What say, hey, gang . . . let's give 'em this one for Jim. One good play. Everyone in it. 86 on 3. Dave, watch that defensive halfback. Jake, fade out a little more. End around direct pass. Everyone got it? Remember, they're scared now. They're plenty worried. And they're just as tired as we are. Ok, gang, let's make this one a good one for Jim."

They went into formation. He leaned over, took the ball, and faded slowly back. Meyer and Bob and Jake ran out ahead to form interference; Ned slipped around and then, going ahead, cut toward the sidelines. Ronald saw a form rushing toward him, dodged, and then let loose. This time he had the whole panorama of the play before his eyes.

The pass was true and straight out to the side. This time Ned was there waiting. Gee, if he only holds it. Cool as ice, the end gathered the ball in, turned and cut across the field behind Jake and Meyer. Someone went down. Gosh, is that Ned? Nope, they're still after him. The pursuit continued. Running forward, Ronny could see scattered bodies writhing on the ground in the mud and mist up ahead. Ned was crossing over now, heading for the opposite sideline. He was in the clear.

A wild spontaneous cheer came from his side. From Abraham Lincoln High.

7

You're sore. Yes, you're plenty sore. And weary. And tired, and lame all over, even a day and a half after that last whistle blew. Sore? Why not? Imagine Keith Davidson, one hundred and eighty pounds of uniform and armor, charging down on you at full speed. He's wearing heavy cleated shoes and considerable extra padding, not to mention a stiff leather helmet that's supposed to protect his skull. Actually it's a first class battering ram, and if it should smack you just right can bash in your nose or break your jaw.

Sore? Yes, you're sore all over; stiff and lame, too. Everything aches, everything. But the aches and pains are forgotten in the warm sensation which comes as you walk down the aisle at assembly in the auditorium between Jim and Meyer. Ronny and Meyer and Jim.

"Nice work, Ronny . . ."

"Hey, Ronny . . ."

"Great going, Meyer, great going, Ronny, nice work there, Jim."

" 'Atsa boy, Jim."

"Yeah, Ronny."

And all the kids slapping at you and reaching for your hand and hollering, and the stiffness gone and the soreness also as you came down the long aisle and sank into your seat with the seniors. The whole auditorium was clapping in steady unison, and the clapping continued while LeRoy walked to his place in front. He was wearing the same badly fitting greenish sweater with the checked shirt underneath. If he felt anything he did not show it. His face was as set and impassive as ever while the school thundered. Gee, that's great, that is. There's the boy who really won things for us; he's a sweetheart, that baby.

Mr. Curry came forward on the platform. Ronny reflected how the Duke would enjoy an after-game scene such as this, what a kick he'd get from standing before the Academy telling his stories, praising the team in well-chosen sentences. Mr. Curry didn't. He began reading a series of announcements in a dry, dull voice, apparently anxious to get it over as soon as possible, to hurry off that platform away from the school to the emptiness of his own room.

"Following members of the team and substitutes will make the trip to Miami a week from Saturday." He began calling off their names; but the cheers after each one were so loud you could hardly catch them even toward the front where Ronny sat. "For faithful work on the scrubs during the past two seasons, Coach Quinn has also decided to take along Jerry Richards and Bob Benedict." More cheers.

"Please pay close attention. The band and fifteen cheerleaders will accompany the squad. The drill squad will be permitted to go on payment of ten dollars apiece toward expenses. Unless at least seventy members of the drill squad sign up, their trip will be canceled." He fumbled with the notes in his hand.

"Any members of the team who wish their parents to go may bring them in the special train. Fare, including hotel expenses in Miami, thirty-seven fifty. Please get in touch with my office. All applications for places must be in by Friday evening. We have to notify the Central Railroad on Saturday morning of the exact number of persons making the trip. The train will leave the Union Depot on Thursday, the 22nd, at 9:45 A.M. and return Monday morning in time for the first period study." Groans rose over the auditorium; titters followed the groans to which he paid no attention. "We shall stay in the Seminole Hotel while in Miami. If you have any questions about the trip, consult Miss Robbins in my office who has charge of arrangements."

They stumbled back up the aisle, the team in a body. That was the coach's idea; in assemblies and the cafeteria he had them all sit together as much as possible. So down the corridor to his homeroom through a welcoming chorus of shouts and yells. It was the same thing in every class. The game! The game against Miami. That was on everyone's mind. No one expected him to be prepared and even Mrs. Taylor looked at him with an understanding gaze.

"No use asking you to translate for us today, I presume, Ronald." He observed that she failed to pick up her little black book as usual, but went right on to the next pupil.

Then after the Latin class it hit him. It hit him and made him reel, as if he had actually been slapped in the face. That was just the way it felt, too. A couple of kids walking behind him in the corridor did it.

"Yeah, but who'll he play in left end?"

"Guess he'll use Stacey's sub, most prob'ly."

Left end! Let's see; why that's Ned's position. Ned LeRoy.

The horrible thought came to him for the first time. Of course. He stood for a minute collecting himself. No, it couldn't be true. They wouldn't do such a thing. Down the corridor came Ned walking slowly, half-smiling as the kids shouted at him. Underneath he was the same quiet, decent boy, waiting as usual to speak until you spoke first.

"Ned! C'm over here." Ned was startled as Ronny hauled him to one side by the lockers. He took him by one shoulder. "Ned! Tell me, tell me straight. You coming down with us, aren't you? I mean, you're playing Intersectional, aren't you?" His heart fell as he watched the big brown eyes look up. There was no change of expression on that passive countenance.

"Nope, Ronald. Guess not."

"Why? Why not? What d'you mean?"

"They don't like to let colored boys play down there, that's all." Then nothing. He said nothing. Ronald couldn't think what to say. Suddenly Ned added, "I sure hope they broadcast that game."

It was this, his simple acceptance of the situation, that made the most impression, that hurt Ronny most of all.

The next period was a study period, and with the excuse that a lame wrist needed taping Ronald went across the hall into the office of the coach near the gym and the lockers. He was sitting at his desk completely surrounded by an ocean of letters and papers.

"Well, Ronald! How you feel this morning? How's that wrist? No bad effects, are there? Sore? Here, let me have a look at it a minute."

"Nosir; no, Coach. I didn't come for that. I came to ask is it true that Ned LeRoy can't play Intersectional?"

The silence seemed to last and last. The coach was looking at him queerly, saying nothing. He nodded. "That's correct, Ronald."

"But, Coach! You know we couldn't have won that game without Ned, you know that, everyone knows that: unless he plays, our forward passing attack is all shot. They can lay for Stacey; they know his sub on the other side is useless catching passes; he's always late." The words poured out fast and faster.

The coach, that hard-bitten gentleman, leaned over and patted him on the shoulder. Ronald recoiled. He had not come for sympathy. He had come for an explanation, for the righting of a wrong. It was a long while coming.

"Take it easy, boy, take it easy. I know all about it. But the fact is they don't permit colored boys to play down there."

"Aw, gee, Coach, we can't play without Ned. Why he won that game for us! Coach, we can't go down there without him."

The coach stood up. "Take it easy, Ronald. This is just one of those things. There isn't anything you or I can do about it. We have to accept the situation. That's life. You see, you can't change human nature. I realize of course that it's tough for Ned; well, sure, it's tough for you, tough for a fine captain like Jim to have to play without one of his reliable men, tough for the whole team. But we can't do anything, so we better just forget it."

Ronald went back bewildered to the class. Maybe Mr. Kates could help. Of all the teachers in Abraham Lincoln High Mr. Kates was the most sensible, the fairest in his marking. So instead of going up to the cafeteria in his lunch period, Ronald stayed down and caught him coming out of the faculty room on the ground floor.

"Mr. Kates, can I speak to you for a minute? See, it's about Ned LeRoy; maybe you heard, Mr. Kates. Yeah. Uhuh. That's right. Ned can't go down, he can't play Intersectional against Miami. It doesn't somehow seem fair to me."

"Fair!" The little man looked at him. There was fire in his voice which was encouraging. "Fair! Naturally not. Who said anything about fairness?"

"Well then, if it isn't fair, there must be something we can do about it."

"What makes you think so?" This wasn't quite so encouraging.

"Mebbe we could . . . mebbe we could insist on playing him. They'd have to let us if we insisted. If we just brought him along."

"H'm. Yes. But would that be pleasant for LeRoy, Ronald?"

"Why, no, I guess it wouldn't. I really hadn't thought of that. But there oughta be something we could do just the same. I wonder isn't there something?"

Yet not even Mr. Kates was much help in this problem. Nor his dad. That evening he was explaining it all to Sandra.

"Now take Dad; he listens and sucks on his pipe and says he understands and all that; he says, sure, it's hard; but what you gonna do about it? They all say the same thing."

"But, Ronny, what could you do?"

"Darned if I know. Only it's so unjust, it's so unfair. Here's Ned, played three years on the team, won goodness knows how many games for the school, and Saturday, well, you saw him out there Saturday. This hurts, Sandra, you understand? I can't exactly explain, but it hurts."

"I know. I understand, Ronny."

"So they reward him by keeping him home. That's his reward. Three years our regular end and about the hottest thing we got in cleats . . . and he's my friend, too, Sandra. You know how you feel when a friend you've been through something important with gets a raw deal."

"It's rotten. What about Mr. Quinn?"

"Onions to him. That's the worst of it, none of the older people seem to mind. They say, sure, it's tough; ok, but what are you going to do about it? They're sorry for him and that's all. The coach is sorry to lose a reliable end and go down there with a sub; but he isn't terribly upset, seems like. He takes it quietly. You know the stuff the older people peddle. Same old line. They tell you how you can't change human nature, so go away and forget all about it."

"It's sick-making. That's what."

"Sure is. He's a member of the team or else he isn't. He's good enough to play against Broadwood and Hillsborough and the Academy and the rest; why isn't he good enough to play against Miami? I don't get it. Y'know, Sandra, here's an idea. I got an idea. I b'lieve if two or three of us made a row, we might do something. Like if Meyer and Jim and me . . ."

"Have you talked to them?"

"Not yet. I only heard about it this noon."

"Why don't you talk to them? I bet they'll feel the same way, they'll think it's rotten, too."

"By gosh, I'll try. We might organize the school if only we could get the kids started. Is there anyone else we could get in on this to help?"

"Yes."

"Who?"

"Me."

"You?"

"Yes, me. I feel it's terrible, the whole thing, just as you do."

"Thanks lots, Sandra. That's pretty swell. But there isn't much a girl can do."

"So you think. Ronald, you don't know this school very well. It isn't like the Academy. Down here the girls help run things and they're important. Also, they're my friends. Like Jessie Stokes, she's the editor of the *Mercury*, and Helen and Lorena, the head cheerleaders. I'll get right after them. Then there are others that are important, and I know 'em all. Meanwhile you get together with Meyer and Jim . . ."

Actually Meyer and Jim were waiting for him as he parked his bike before the school the next morning. They looked worried. Their first words showed they were all worried about the same thing.

"We called you up last night. Have you heard about Ned LeRoy?"

"Yeah. I heard yesterday. It's rotten, isn't it? What we gonna do?"

"We oughta do something."

"We oughta get up a petition."

"We oughta see Mr. Curry and . . ."

"We oughta call a meeting of the Student Council . . ."

"No, here's what we oughta do, we oughta . . ."

"Look here, first off, couldn't we have a talk with the coach?"

"Nuts to that. I spoke to him yesterday."

"Wha'd he say?"

"Same old line. Can't do anything . . ."

Inside the first bell rang and the sound came faintly to their ears.

"Look, we've got to move quick. Let's us three have a meeting first of all. We'll get together at lunch instead of going upstairs."

"OK with me."

"I'll be there."

"All right. Outside the room when the second lunch bell rings . . ."

II

"Attention, please!" As the voice of the principal came over the loudspeaker above Mr. Kates' head, the teacher ceased talking. The dullish tones continued. "There will be a meeting of the football squad directly after school. That is all."

Once school was dismissed for the day, a feeling of a thunderstorm hung in the air. Classrooms and corridors buzzed and hummed, the building quivered with excitement. Not merely the excitement of the projected journey; but the excitement of clash and conflict. In a day and a half a sharp division in the student body had become apparent. On one side were the majority who were in favor of the trip; who were on the squad, the band, or the drill team, besides those who wanted to go even if they couldn't. On the other side was the small knot against it, led by Ronny and Meyer and Jim. In the halls and on the stairs and by opened lockers groups of intense boys and girls surrounded every supporter of canceling the Miami trip.

On his way to the locker room, Ronald found the coach waiting at his door. He called him in and shut it, making Ronald feel almost like a prisoner at the bar.

"Ronald! What's all this nonsense about? First I heard was last night—yesterday afternoon. Seems a few of you boys are trying hard to upset our game with Miami."

Ronald squirmed. That must be the way it looked to an outsider. "Well, Coach, a few of us are pretty upset about Ned LeRoy: Meyer and Jim and me."

"But I thought I explained all that to you day before yesterday. You're up against life now. In life there are certain situations which we all have to accept."

"Uhuh. Yessir. We're planning to talk it over this afternoon. That's the reason Jim called the squad together."

"There's nothing to talk over. We can't back out of this game now. You must realize we'd be letting the Miami team down if we failed to show up. Think of it; the game has been officially scheduled for over a week, they've sold something like ten thousand tickets, printed programs, and spent hundreds of dollars getting ready for us. What is there to talk over?"

Ronny was silent. This he had never fully considered, neither had Meyer nor Jim. But then, all Miami had to do was let LeRoy compete. Besides, he felt in a strong position. This was his last year of football, his final game. No penalties could be swung against him if he refused to play.

"Now see here, Ronald, I want you to go in there and explain things to the rest of the boys. You have a great influence with the team, coming the way you do from the outside, and then you're older than most of them. They'll take a lot from you, they'll follow your lead."

I only hope they will, he thought. "Afraid I can't do that, Coach."

"Why not?"

" 'Cause I think we oughtn't to go to Miami without Ned."

"You mean to say you'd . . . you mean to stand there and look me in the face and tell me you'd wreck . . . you'd ruin our chances against Miami . . . now look here, get one thing clear. What you propose doing is insubordination. Insubordination to school discipline. We're going down to play Miami. If you don't care to go along, that's your affair. I'll slap Jack Train in your place. We don't need you, we don't need to win, we've never needed victory so much we had to go back on our principles in this school. Just fix that in your mind."

He was angry. Recalling his talk on the opening day of practice, and having sat on the bench beside him through several games, Ronald realized how little truth there was in his remarks. He let him bluster on but refused to promise a thing. Yet he didn't like the position; insubordination was an ugly word.

The coach raved and stormed and threatened but gradually saw he was getting nowhere. Before long Ronny was in the locker room, the gang ready and awaiting his arrival. There they were, Jim and Mike and Don and Vic and Bob and Meyer, subs and all. Many still bore tangible evidence of Saturday's battle. Jim was hobbling round with a cane. Meyer had a taped gash above his eye where he had been cut. Dave's leg was stuck out stiff and straight from the bench on which he sat. Mike had his right arm in a sling, and several others bore patches of plaster across their cheeks. Everyone was there save LeRoy.

"Hi, Ronny. We're waiting for you," said Jim. "Now let's see, men, how'll we go about this? Suppose first of all you tell the gang how you feel, Ronald."

He stood up beside Jim before the two rows of benches. "Well, gee, fellows, it's something like this. You all know the facts just as well as I do. We've been invited to play Intersectional against Miami High. They don't allow colored boys to compete on their teams, so Coach intends we should leave Ned home. I think it's a dirty trick, especially on a player like Ned."

He stopped and nobody spoke. Everyone in the room felt the coming crisis but no one felt like bringing it to the front. The silence became embarrassing. One sub blurted out, "Aw, so what? What can we do?"

They all looked at Ronald who looked back at them; at Mike and Dave who'd made the holes for him all fall, at Don who'd faced and outplayed the best center the Academy had ever had, at all that crowd who'd taken a beating so he could help score the winning touchdown in the game. Good kids, most of them. Yet disturbed more by the possible sacrifice of the trip than by an injustice done to a team member.

"Look, you guys. How would you feel? Suppose you'd been on the team three years and given all you've got. You've won the game against the Academy after we were licked and beaten. Then they tell you that you can't play Intersectional. Is that right? Is that a decent thing?"

"You can't very well change human nature, Ronny," piped a voice from the back bench.

He was disgusted. "Aw, you heard your old man say that last night."

"Did not."

"Did so."

"Look, I think we oughta . . ."

"Seems to me if we could . . ."

"Gosh, kids, can't you see, don't you understand?" He looked round at some of their faces, obstinate, mulish, mouths set, many of them frowning already at the thought of giving up the Miami trip. Why, some of these kids are as bad as the older folks, he thought. As bad as the kids at the Academy.

"It's tough on Ned, but what can we do?"

"Sure, what can *we* do?"

It angered him. "I'll tell you. Here's what we can do. We can all refuse to go to Miami."

The thunder rumbled. There was lightning in the air. A flash. Another flash. Silence before the storm. Then it burst. Everybody was talking at once, all together; soon they were yelling, shouting. Their indifference had vanished. The storm had swept over them and drenched everybody.

Ronald watched. He knew the ones who were anxious to go like Mike and Jake Smith and one or two subs, the ones who were more or less uncertain like Vic and Bob, and the two staunch ones who would stand beside him. They'd stand together, the three of them—Ronny and Meyer and Jim.

Right then Jim came to his rescue. He rose. "As captain of the team, I'd like to offer a suggestion."

"Hey, you guys, shut up, listen . . ."

"Keep quiet, fellas . . ."

"Listen a minute, will ya?"

"It's just this. We all know now a lot's involved in this in many ways. I think the fair thing for us to do would be go home and think about it carefully overnight, and then come back and hold a meeting tomorrow after school to vote on this question. Isn't that the best way?"

Good for Jim. He could see that Jim feared bringing it to a vote at that moment, that he hoped some could be persuaded to vote with them by the next afternoon. Mentally he checked over the members of the team and the subs of whom the two chosen were also eligible to vote. It looked bad. It sure looked bad. The kids just didn't want to give up the trip for a principle.

For nothing; that's what it seemed like to most of them.

They went down the deserted corridors, still arguing among themselves, when there was a flutter of feet on stone and a feminine voice behind them. "Perry!" It was Miss Robbins from the principal's office. "Mr. Curry would like to see you a minute, and Stacey and Goldman, too, please." They turned, went back down the hall, and as they passed through the outer office Ronny recognized Jack Malone, sports editor of the *Courier*, sitting on one of the benches reading a magazine. This was really getting hot.

Within was a solemn group. As he was introduced, Ronald remembered one man, a friend of his dad's. It was Mr. Swift, the president of the Trust Company whom he had not seen since that day at the station. The other man he knew by name, everyone in town knew his name. Henry J. Latham was the head of the pump factory, and he had often heard him mentioned by his father. People in town spoke of Mr. Latham in tones of gratitude, dislike, affection, and dismay. He was president of the Chamber of Commerce, active in business, and the political boss of the city.

They got away to a rapid start. Mr. Curry

spoke first. "Ronald, these gentlemen are somewhat upset about our plans for the coming trip to Miami. You've been on the team, and you've been prominent in the whole thing; suppose you tell them your story."

Yes, this was certainly getting hot. First the *Courier*, then Mr. Swift, and now old man Latham. The bank and the Chamber of Commerce. He looked at Jim and Meyer. They looked back, approval in their faces, and he saw he had them behind him. Ronny and Meyer and Jim. Well, here goes. Here's the works.

"There isn't much to tell, sir. This is our point of view. Y'see, sir, we feel, that is Jim and Meyer and I . . . and one or two others . . . we feel on the team it's pretty darn hard luck on Ned LeRoy, his not getting a chance to go in against Miami next week."

Mr. Latham, white-haired, well dressed like Mr. Swift, explained patiently. "My boy, aren't you Rob Perry's son? I thought so. Well now, I think I can explain this to you. It seems they don't permit colored players to compete down there."

"Yessir, I know all that, sir. Only we don't hafta play them, do we?"

Then Mr. Swift broke in. "You surely wouldn't want them to break a law of their State just for us, would you, boys?" He looked from one to the other and back again, at Ronny and then at Meyer and at Jim. Ronald hardly knew what to say. He hadn't realized it was a law. Maybe if it was a law they couldn't do anything. Then Meyer saved him as he had often done on the field.

"Are you sure it's a law, Mr. Swift?"

He got no answer. Mr. Swift brushed the question aside. "These are all technicalities. But I'll answer that question of Perry's. Yes, I'm rather afraid we *do* have to play them. You see, a thing of this kind isn't arranged overnight. It takes considerable planning. Now this special train, for instance. Do you boys realize that four to five hundred businessmen from town are going down just to support you on the field? Know what that means? It means about thirty cars—diners, sleepers, club cars, lounges, baggage cars, and so on. You can't throw a train like that together in an hour. There's a good many thousand dollars involved in a thing of this sort. D'you understand, boys?"

The boys understood. Mr. Latham then added

his angle. He was, Ronald decided, just another old smoothie. Why was it older folks got that way? "Let me ask you a question, Perry. Do you think it's better to disappoint one colored boy or forty thousand people?"

"How d'you mean, sir?"

"It's simple. The entire town is heart and soul behind this team. Five hundred citizens putting up their own money to go down to Miami. Moreover the Chamber of Commerce has voted enough cash to enable the drill team to go along at a minimum expense. Now . . ."

Mr. Swift, on the edge of his chair, interrupted. Their anxiety over the thing was plain enough, for neither would let the other finish a sentence.

"Last year we outfitted the band completely. We're proud of this school. We think it's the best high school in the State. We're proud of the team. Naturally you wouldn't want to do anything to hurt the town, would you? Of course not." He smiled a fishy kind of smile. Ronald disliked him. He looked at Meyer and Jim and could see they disliked him also. Well, he thought, we're sticking together.

Mr. Latham continued his argument. "I said

just now it was a question of disappointing one colored boy or forty thousand people in town. Maybe I should have said a hundred and sixty thousand folks here in the County who want to see you go down there and clean up those Southern crackers."

It was hard to laugh off, three boys against a hundred and sixty thousand people. Yet he knew it was untrue, he felt it was not so but he couldn't explain it away. Then help came from an unexpected source.

"I wonder . . . I wonder whether we are being quite straight with these boys." The soft-voiced man behind the desk, who so far hadn't said a word, spoke up.

"What do you mean, straight?" Mr. Latham was angry now. He was almost snarling. "The game's been scheduled. All arrangements have been made with the Central Railroad, all the tickets have been sold. We have to consider the Miami people, you know. We can't put them in a hole; we have responsibilities toward them."

"That's right," echoed Mr. Swift with enthusiasm in his voice. "We have a great responsibility toward our opponents. Fair play. Give the other man a chance. That's one of the elements of sportsmanship. Sportsmanship; must be good sports, you know." He looked around for approval.

"True." The tone was quiet, almost monotonous. "True, but isn't our first responsibility toward these boys here?" Ronald was amazed at the little man's persistence. That mild figure behind the desk changed in his eyes; he really had what it takes; he was a fighter after all. And he was for them, on their side, not against them as some principals would have been in his place.

Ronny looked at his friends, at Meyer and Jim. They were looking toward the man behind the desk and he knew they felt just the way he did.

"Our real, our only responsibility, it seems to me, is to these boys. They should do whatever they think is right. After all, it's their game, isn't it?"

No one spoke. The atmosphere suddenly became tense. The two businessmen looked outraged. One could see they were used to having their own way and had expected it that afternoon.

"See here, Mr. Latham. Mind if I ask you a question?" As he said it Ronald wondered at his own audacity. He saw the open-mouthed faces of Meyer and Jim looking at him, the grim visage of the man across the room. Well, here goes. They can't do any more than kill me. Everyone turned his way, the president of the Chamber of Commerce, the head of the Trust Company, the principal of the school, and his two friends and teammates.

"Mind if I ask you one question? This is the Abraham Lincoln High. D'you think . . . d'you guess Abraham Lincoln would like this? Would he say ok, leaving a colored boy off our team when we go to Miami?"

Nobody replied. Then the president of the Trust Company rose. So did the other man. "My boy, when you get a little older you won't be so hotheaded, you'll understand better how these problems work out. We can't change society overnight. We just have to accept certain injustices and make the best of it. You've been told how much money is involved in all this, and how the reputation of the town is at stake. I tell you what I'm going to do."

He hesitated a moment and then placed one hand on Jim's shoulder and the other on Meyer's. Was it because he was nearer to them or did he feel that Ronald was hopeless?

"I tell you what I'm going to do. I'm going to put this thing right up to you. I'm going to trust you boys to do the right thing in the end."

III

When, on his return from school, his mother informed him that his father wished to see him downtown, he realized there was trouble ahead. He was sure of it when Miss Jessup in the outer office told him to go right in. He was expected.

From the desk where he sat his father looked up. "Ah! There you are, Ronald. Look here, what's all this mess about the trip to Miami? Seems as if I've heard nothing else all day long. Please tell me about the whole thing, beginning at the beginning."

"Why, Dad! We talked it all over. You know about it. I explained it to you night before last."

"I know you did, but I'm ashamed to say I didn't pay a lot of attention. These Intersectional games between high schools are something new since my day."

"Well, it's just this. We've had an offer to play an Intersectional game against Miami High. Only we can't use Ned LeRoy because he's colored. So Meyer and Jim and I, we feel it's unfair. See, Dad, Ned's a right guy, and we don't want to go without him. The whole team meets tomorrow to vote on whether or not we'll go. Some of the kids want to go, some of us don't."

"And you're leading the group who don't want to go, is that it?"

There was a kind of note of accusation in his voice. Ronny shifted in his chair. Was he going to have his own dad against him, too? Gee, this was really getting tough. "Uhuh. Yes, Dad, I suppose so."

"I see." The telephone rang. He picked it up. "Who? Who? Oh, yes. All right, put him on. Hullo . . . hullo, Ed. How are you? Not at all. No bother at all. Why, yes, I do. Yes, he's right here now in the office with me. Yes, I presume he is . . . ha, ha . . . well, ha, ha . . . he's a good boy . . . did he . . . did he? . . ." He winked at Ronald.

"Oh, yes, I know. Yes, he's just been talking to me about it. H'm . . . yes . . . yes . . . I see . . . yes . . . that is awkward, isn't it? I know all that, Ed, but . . . well, Ed, I agree with you; but I'm bound to say I do understand the boy's angle on this whole thing. What's that?

Well, I'll be glad to talk to him . . . certainly I'll talk to him, but I'm not sure I'll change his point of view . . . yes, I'll be happy to do all I can, but of course in the end he must act as he thinks best . . . I say he must decide for himself . . . yes, I do . . . yes, I will, yes . . . thank you . . . good-bye . . .

"Whew! That's what it's been like all day long. Ronald, my boy, seems as if you've rather started something in town. D'ja see the editorial in this afternoon's *Courier*? Take a look." He handed over the folded newspaper. The front editorial was headed:

"BOLSHEVISM IN HIGH SCHOOL?

"We understand that the proposed trip of the football team for the Intersectional game against Miami High School which has been scheduled for a week from Saturday is being threatened by a small band of revolutionary students at Abraham Lincoln. Fortunately their number and influence is small; but the mere existence of the movement jeopardizes both the success of the trip and the victory of our team on the field." As he read down the column Ronald became hotter and hotter, angrier and angrier. "It appears that these young persons do not believe the trip is being handled in a way they like, and claim an injustice is being done to one member of the squad.

"It is quite evident that manners are not being taught in our public schools today, for these young persons appear to forget that we are going as the guests of the Miami High School. As such we have the obligation to act like guests and abide by the customs obtaining in that city. Already many older people here in town have spent considerable time, energy, and money toward helping the success of the journey. Over a thousand dollars has been voluntarily subscribed by supporters of the eleven to permit the band of forty pieces and the fifteen cheerleaders to make the journey, while the larger part of the expenses of the drill team has also been collected. In view of this fact, and also that between five and six hundred townspeople have signed up with the Central Railroad to make the trip at their own cost merely to support the team in action, we hope the young recalcitrants will come to their senses, and quickly."

•

"But, Dad! Look! That isn't right. That isn't it at all. That isn't right what that man says there."

"Don't worry, Ronald." He laughed. "Don't worry about that. I know the background of this. Mr. Swift's bank, the Trust Company, has a mortgage of half a million on the *Courier* plant. Old Jamison, the editor, will write anything the bank wants. That means what Swift wants. He wants to have the trip because he—or the bank, or both—is tied up in a lot of real estate that was unloaded on them during the depression. He thinks the trip will be a good advertisement for the town. Pay no attention to it. But just the same, I wonder whether you hadn't better think seriously . . ."

The telephone jangled. In an exasperated tone he replied. "Yes? Who? Latham? Why, yes, put him on. Hullo, Henry." It was old man Latham, that smoothie! Gee, they were on Dad hot and heavy, weren't they? Ronny wondered whether Jim's and Meyer's fathers were under pressure like this, too.

"Well, Henry, I think . . . yes I do . . . by all means . . . why, Henry . . . what's that? . . . the railway stands to lose ten thousand if the trip's canceled? Does . . . whew! Yes, but the kid seems to think . . . you do . . . oh, good, I'd welcome a solution; frankly, I'm . . . no I don't much like the whole thing myself . . .

"What's that? A hundred dollars. A hundred dollars to him? Oh, no, I don't like that at all . . . looks too much like a bribe to me . . . no . . . nope, sorry . . . well, yes, I'll be glad to tell Ronald . . . yes, he's a good boy . . . oh, did he? . . . did he really!" There was an amused laugh, and another wink. "Well, good enough. That's fine. Yes, I do, I see your position in the matter perfectly . . . certainly, Henry, I'll talk to him, but he must do whatever he thinks best . . . how's that? What's that?" His face flushed suddenly. "What's that . . . look here, you aren't hinting, you aren't suggesting, are you?" Ronald had never seen his dad quite like this before. He leaned into the telephone. "Oh, all right. All right then, Henry. Yes, I'll talk it over with him. Yes. Good-bye." He was curt, short. He placed the receiver down with a sharp gesture.

"Aha! This really goes deep. One of our best clients is the Central Railroad. We've done all their work in the County for almost fifteen years.

Now Henry Latham is hinting or suggesting, or whatever you want to call it, that if the Miami trip is canceled the railway will lose so much money they'll have to take the account elsewhere."

"You mean, Dad, he'd try to get you to make me change that way?"

"Oh, no. He's much too smart to say so. He knows it would make me mad. Just his hints at it made me angry. This thing has really gone deep, though, I confess. I had no real understanding of what was at stake the other night when you spoke about the trip."

Nor yet had Ronald. He was solemn now. It started, how? Why, just between Ned LeRoy and himself. The forward passing combination of the Abraham Lincoln team. Then Meyer and Jim were in on it, and then the coach, and then the principal, and now it was dragging in all sorts of people and things; railways, bank presidents, Chambers of Commerce, newspapers, political bosses; why, it was even reaching into Dad's own business.

His father swung round in the swivel chair. Looking out of the window with his back toward Ronald, he said:

"My boy, you've attacked something. Without knowing it, without the least intention in the world, you've attacked something. You've attacked one of the injustices of our American democracy. You've also attacked indirectly the commercialism of sport. And whenever you attack anything of that kind, you always find someone behind who's making money from it."

Now Ronny saw. He understood, he realized something of the forces against them. His father continued. "He won't get far that way with me. I rather imagine he knows it, too. We're fighters, you and I, Ronald; we don't scare easy. I guess you've got something of your dad in you. I confess now that I'm beginning to think somewhat as you do. Here's old man Latham's suggestion. Seems they, that is the crowd running the whole show—Swift and Latham and the rest—have offered Ned LeRoy a hundred dollars to buy some clothes if he stays home. What do you think of that?"

He was shocked. He was shocked and he was wounded; the idea hurt. "Oh, no, Dad! Why he's a right guy, Ned is. He only wants to play against Miami. He isn't interested in a hundred dollars, Dad."

"Don't like it, do you? Good. Neither do I. Glad it hits you that way, Ronald." The telephone rang. He turned and put his hand over the receiver, and before he replied, said: "This is the way it's been all day long. I haven't done a lick since nine this morning. Everyone in town has been on me because of you and this Miami trip." He picked up the receiver. "Yes? Who? Oh, yes . . ."

He did the strangest thing. Putting the receiver back, he rose and strode into the outer office. Ronald watched him in amazement, heard his voice greeting somebody. In a minute he returned with a stranger. The stranger, short, dark, with black hair and glasses, had a cigar in one hand. He greeted Ronald like an old friend, seizing his hand and congratulating him on his play in the Academy game. Then Ronny recognized the man. It was Meyer's father, the head of Goldman and Straus, Gent's Furnishings and Clothes.

"Sit down. Sit down, Mr. Goldman. Sit down, we're right in the middle of the thing. I was just saying to my boy here they've been on my neck all day long. First one person then another."

"Same here. What's this about, anyhow? Folks

downtown been dropping into the store all day, telling me my boy is trying to spoil the football trip to Miami. Mr. Perry, you wouldn't believe . . ."

"Oh, yes, I would. I've had 'em in here . . ."

"But the whole town is after me now. I'm right there on Main Street, easy to get at. What's it all about, that they should make such a fuss over a football game, Mr. Perry? You wouldn't believe the things they've told me."

"Yes, they're anxious, all right."

"The Trust Company calls up and tells me how I'd better make sure Meyer gets to go on the trip, or else, they hint, they might foreclose on our mortgage. I can pay that off, but it isn't easy to find a good place like that corner there on Main and State Streets. I got mad, Mr. Perry, when he said that. I got real mad."

"No wonder. They tried pressure on me, too. Most likely on young Stacey's father also. Maybe you'd better explain what it's all about to Mr. Goldman, Ronald."

"It's simply this, Mr. Goldman. You saw the Academy game. You saw that colored boy, Ned LeRoy, our left end. Well, now it seems if we go down to Miami he can't play."

"Ah . . . sooo . . ." His large black eyebrows rose.

"No. And Meyer and Jim and me, why, we think it's unfair to leave him up here, that it's a dirty trick to do a thing like that."

"Ah . . ."

His father interrupted. "Let me say that at first I felt the boys' position was untenable. I felt they were bucking the inevitable, so to speak; that it was hard luck on everyone concerned, but something you couldn't hope to change. I felt they were all wrong to make an issue of it. Well, they've made me change my mind, the boys have, and these people downtown, too. All day long they've been on my neck from one source or another."

"Oh, but Mr. Perry, you're up here on the eighth floor. I'm down there at the corner of Main and State. Everybody drops in, it's just a corner store." The cigar waggled in Mr. Goldman's hand.

"Well, they've been after me. The Chamber of Commerce. The railway. The Trust Company. Then Latham called, and got my dander up. He hinted the Central might take their work over to Steele's office. Worse, he said the boys around town had made up a purse for young LeRoy.

Seems they're going to give him a hundred bucks so he won't mind missing the trip."

"Oh, that's bad." The cigar waggled again.

"Y'see, Mr. Goldman, he doesn't want the money. He only wants a square deal. He's a right guy, see?"

"Yes, I see. I understand. I'm glad I came over. Meyer's hardly had a chance to explain things to me like this."

"And, Mr. Goldman, we're going to vote on it tomorrow morning. The whole team'll meet and vote whether we go or not. Meyer and Jim Stacey and I, we'll vote together. We stand together, and there's one or two others on our side, too."

"Ok." The black-haired man stood up quickly. His sudden movement shot cigar ashes over the rug. "That's fine. Meyer, he'll stand with you, no matter what happens, I can promise you that. Mr. Perry, glad I saw you. Never mind the business; if they throw me out of that corner, Goldman and Straus will move uptown. We'll find a good spot somewhere. Good-bye. Glad I had this talk with you." He turned to Ronald.

"By ginger, young fellow, you've got something there. Don't let 'em talk you out of it."

IV

They came trooping into the auditorium. Seniors down front, juniors behind them, sophomores in the rear, freshmen in the balcony. Everyone connected with Abraham Lincoln was there; the teachers, all of them, even Miss Rollins of home economics who never went to rallies, the coaches, and Mike, the janitor, with his two helpers. Everyone in school except the team.

The auditorium boiled and bubbled with noise, with arguments between the two factions. From her seat up front Sandra watched the excited mob, turbulent and aroused, those who were angry about what they felt was a wrong, and those—it was the larger number, she knew— who saw a fine trip ruined by a gang of hotheads.

She glanced round. Everyone was there except the team. Finally they entered. From their faces as they came down the aisle it was impossible to tell the result of the vote. There were Bob and Dave and Mike Fronzak lumbering along, and Vic Snow and Ned LeRoy. Ned wore the same faded greenish sweater with his checked shirt underneath. Last of all came the three of them together; Ronny and Meyer and Jim.

The school rose and cheered and clapped. Sandra rose with the rest but she did not feel like cheering.

Mr. Curry stepped out from behind the red curtains to the front of the platform. He had a slip of white paper in his hand, most likely the slip with the vote, the slip with the fatal news. There it was, and only Mr. Curry and the team knew the result.

He began in his usual way, just as if this was an ordinary meeting, as if nothing at all was at stake, as if this was just like every other assembly throughout the year.

"We will begin as is customary by the singing of the National Anthem."

Rumble. Rattle. Books dropping. The clatter of hundreds of seats. The noise of twelve hundred boys and girls rising. The band started. Some of them, Sandra observed, were really singing as if it mattered, as they didn't usually. The verse ended. Rumble. Rattle. Books dropping. The clatter of hundreds of seats. The noise of twelve hundred boys and girls sitting down again.

Then an immense quiet settled over the auditorium, over the kids and the teachers and the coach and his assistants and Mike, the janitor, and his two helpers standing back there under the balcony in the rear. Everyone was there and everyone was interested. He began. Here it comes. This is it. Here's the sixty-four-dollar question. Will the team go to Miami?

No! Shoot! It wasn't the thing they wanted to know at all. He was only reading notices from the slip in his hand. Aw, heck!

"Mrs. Lewis' sophomore girls club will have a discussion on table manners in the cafeteria tomorrow afternoon at three. All interested are invited."

A low series of groans greeted this. Now isn't it like that icicle! Imagine! A discussion of table manners when we want to know do we go to Miami. Jeepers!

"The girl's intramural basketball series will be started this afternoon in the gymnasium at three-thirty." More groans, slightly more perceptible this time. When would that drip ever get down to business? What about Miami? Are we going to Miami to play Intersectional or aren't we?

Still more routine. "The following officers of clubs have been elected for the coming year. Mathematics club: Jean Wrigley. Senior dramatics club: John Stanswyck. Camera club: Henry

Werman. Radio club: Tom Slater. Bowling club: Barbara Haynes."

Who cares? Who cares about the camera club? Come on, there! Give us the bad news. What about Miami? Are we going to play Intersectional at Miami or aren't we?

"I have a report to make to the student body about the proposed trip to Miami for the suggested football game with the Miami High School." The groans stopped suddenly, the shuffling and whispering died away; utter, complete silence fell over the whole auditorium. Here it comes.

"Due to complications that have arisen, Fosdick-Masten High of Buffalo, New York, has been chosen to make the journey in our place."

A roar broke out. You couldn't tell whether it was approval or disapproval or both. Cheers mingled with groans. The entire auditorium seethed. Anybody however could see that the majority were disappointed at the action taken. He held up his hand for silence.

But silence did not come immediately. The tumult died away slowly; it was a ripple, then a murmur. At last quiet came again. "I have another announcement to make. Late last night Coach Quinn received a telegram challenging us to an Intersectional game a week from Saturday with Oak Park High of Chicago, Illinois. . . ."

Why, you never heard such a yell. It was like nothing at any victory meeting, at any pep rally, like nothing the auditorium had ever heard. They were frantic, boys, girls, the team; yes, even Mike and his assistants in the rear under the balcony.

He couldn't restrain them nor quiet down the noise. They yelled and yelled and yelled some more. As the wave of sound subsided it would burst out again. At last, after waiting, he managed to get order. But this time there was no quiet; a buzz persisted over the entire hall. Everyone had questions to ask of everyone else. Would I get to go? Would you? Would the band be taken? Would the drill team go along? Would . . .

"The same arrangements made for the Miami trip will hold for this trip to Chicago." Another mighty outburst rose. That's super, that is! We're going to Chicago to play Intersectional!

The noise died away as he spoke again. "I'm happy to be able to inform you . . ." he talked slowly and very, very distinctly . . . "that the whole team will go."

Boom! Boom-boom! Boom went the bass drum.

Clash went the cymbals, clash-clash. Then the sounds of the band were lost in the uproar. The band got up, they started along the aisle playing, they were surrounded by yelling kids.

For Abraham Lincoln High was playing Intersectional! The whole team!

Other books in the Odyssey series:

L. M. Boston
- ☐ THE CHILDREN OF GREEN KNOWE
- ☐ TREASURE OF GREEN KNOWE
- ☐ THE RIVER AT GREEN KNOWE
- ☐ AN ENEMY AT GREEN KNOWE
- ☐ A STRANGER AT GREEN KNOWE

Edward Eager
- ☐ HALF MAGIC
- ☐ KNIGHT'S CASTLE
- ☐ MAGIC BY THE LAKE
- ☐ MAGIC OR NOT?
- ☐ SEVEN-DAY MAGIC

Mary Norton
- ☐ THE BORROWERS

John R. Tunis
- ☐ THE KID FROM TOMKINSVILLE
- ☐ WORLD SERIES
- ☐ ALL-AMERICAN
- ☐ YEA! WILDCATS!
- ☐ A CITY FOR LINCOLN

Virginia Hamilton
- ☐ A WHITE ROMANCE
- ☐ JUSTICE AND HER BROTHERS
- ☐ DUSTLAND
- ☐ THE GATHERING

Look for these titles and others in the Odyssey series in your local bookstore.

Or send prepayment in the form of a check or money order to: HBJ (Operator J) 465 S. Lincoln Drive, Troy, Missouri 63379.

Or call: 1-800-543-1918 (ask for Operator J).

☐ I've enclosed my check payable to Harcourt Brace Jovanovich.

Charge my: ☐ Visa ☐ MasterCard
　　　　　　☐ American Express

_____
Card Expiration Date

| | | | | | | | | | | | | | | | | | | |
Card #

_____
Signature

_____
Name

_____
Address

_____
City　　　　　State　　　Zip

Please send me _____ copy/copies @ $3.95 each

($3.95 x no. of copies)　　$_____

Subtotal　　　　　　　　$_____

Your state sales tax　　+ $_____

Shipping and handling　+ $_____
($1.50 x no. of copies)

Total　　　　　　　　　$_____

PRICES SUBJECT TO CHANGE